Desire for You

ISLAND EMBERS, Book 2

Welcome to Silent Whisper

CHERYL BARTON

Dedication

For my dad, John A. Barton, Jr. and my brother, John A. Barton, III, I miss you both every day.

Cotton, you never got the chance to celebrate my journey into writing. I hope I'm making you proud.

To my dad, oh how I miss you being here, my biggest and greatest supporter, in partnership with Mom. Thanks for continuing to watch over me. As you already know, as far as my writing, I can't stop, I won't stop! I'm all in!

Love, *ME!*

Acknowledgements

To my family, friends, supporters and readers, I appreciate you. Thanks for always rocking hard for and with me! I am because of you.

Cheryl

About the *Island Embers* Series:

Join me on this journey into a new sexy, romantic series called, Island Embers. How, do you ask, would embers be used to describe something like a budding romance when its definition means something that's burning away, fading even? Well, that's true, but in this series, embers signify a place where love and desire, which could be fading, flourish again as the embers are ignited hotter and fiercer than ever.

In this series of three books, *Hunger for You*, *Desire for You* and *Thirst for You*, three brothers, Tellum, Byrum and Callum Blackstone have enjoyed their lives as bachelors, never thinking that there would be a woman for each of them who could stoke the desires of their hearts as they do their bodies.

In the business of building romantic resorts, *Secret Whisper*, *Silent Whisper*, and *Quiet Whisper*, each brother will discover that the heart wants what it wants. Their lives are no longer only about intoxicating, lust-filled needs. The grown and sexy in them have found it's about everlasting love.

Thanks for joining me in this second helping of the series with, *Desire for You*. This is Byrum Blackstone's road to everlasting love.

About - Silent Whisper, Book 2

Byrum Blackstone is considered the one Blackstone brother who could not be tamed by any woman, no matter how salaciously desirable she is. That is, until he finds himself vulnerable to the one woman he should stay far away from; his executive assistant, Keiko Lee.

In the midst of fighting for her freedom and for custody of her son, Keiko vows to never trust another man with her heart. What she didn't expect was for her boss to offer her wicked, blood pressure spiking, hotter than she's ever known before nights of passion that stir her body and her heart back to life.

Neither Byrum nor Keiko are willing to admit their true feelings as the bigger problem of losing their careers overshadows how bittersweet newfound love could be not just in the present, but in the foreseeable future.

Welcome to Silent Whisper!

From the ending of *Hunger for You*,
Book 1 of the Island Embers series

The wedding reception of
Tellum and Cheyenne Blackstone

The wedding reception for Tellum and Cheyenne Blackstone was in full swing. An exquisite menu accompanied by live music and an even livelier crowd of two hundred guests, Byrum was having the time of his life. On a warm June day, months after his brother proposed to the love of his life, their closest family members and friends were gathered for the event of the year in downtown Detroit. The wedding had taken place over an hour ago in the same venue, keeping guests from having to travel from one location to another for the wedding and then the reception. Thankfully, both occurred at a five-star hotel that accommodated everyone to spend at least one night at the hotel.

Byrum leaned back in his chair at the head table where he sat next to Tellum on one side and on the other was one of Cheyenne's friends, who was one of two maids-of-honor. The other, her best friend Melodi, sat on the other side of Callum who sat next to Cheyenne. The rest of the wedding party were seated at three tables near the head table. He was still floored that Tellum and Cheyenne had ten groomsmen, not including him and Callum, and the same number of bridesmaids. This was one of the biggest wedding's he had ever been to or a part of. He shouldn't be surprised that his brother and his bride would go all out on their big day. Their love was as big and magnificent as the event was.

The food had been served, the cake had been cut and most

of what kept him at the reception had surpassed. He was ready to head out to a space that was just him. He needed a night to relax and get his thoughts in check. For now, there is no place he would rather be than right here as Tellum's right-hand man. Then he thought about it and realized there was one place that would appease him a little more. His eyes cut to a table on the far left of the dance floor. For three months, he'd self-tortured himself by being close to a woman that he couldn't have, though she was all he wanted. Trying to avoid anyone seeing him ogling her, he lifted his drink to his mouth and sipped it slowly. He was hoping to hide where his eyes were focused. They were locked in on Keiko Lee, his executive assistant.

A few months back, he and his team had finally and easily settled into the company-provided accommodations on the private island in the Mediterranean that would be the home of the brothers' next resort, *Silent Whisper*. It hadn't always been his plan to make the island his home, but with so much work to be done and with this resort being his baby, he made the sacrifice to move to the island pretty much full-time. He made trips back to Detroit and other locations for business purposes, but most of his time was spent on the island. He didn't realize how much he needed a break from Detroit until he did. Not only was he on the island, but so was Keiko with her exotic looks. She was an incredibly beautiful woman who heritage came from her African American father and Asian mother.

Keiko was five-foot-nine with the longest, sexiest legs in the history of women. She had long, thick black as coal hair that cascaded down her back. Her full lips had a permanent look of being thoroughly kissed. Gorgeous black as midnight eyes had a magnetism that made him want to stare into them without the need to ever look away. He did when he thought others may see his obvious, startling attraction to her; his insatiable desire for her. Coming home for the wedding, he had hoped that distance from her would help to reign in his longing to have her in his arms and in his bed. That wasn't to be.

One day, he and Keiko were talking in her office about his travel plans to return to the Detroit for the wedding and she mentioned she was also heading home. She couldn't wait to spend some quality time with her son who was staying with his father while she worked and lived on the island full-time. When she paused in explaining her reason for going home, he caught a weird expression on her face as if she were leaving something out that may be uncomfortable to reveal. When he asked her about it, she told him that she'd received an invitation to Tellum and Cheyenne's wedding. He knew that she and Cheyenne were acquaintances but didn't know that they were close enough for the small group that were invited to the wedding. He didn't question it, but instead, told her he was happy that she was going. Most of all, he was overjoyed that she would get the chance to see her son whom everyone knew she missed. Tru, five years old, was the light of her life. Her ex-husband, DeConnor, let Tru video chat with her every day; sometimes more than once a day. After months of intense angst while going through their divorce, she and DeConnor were finally in a good communicative space after they agreed it would be best for their son to stay in the states.

Twice a month, on the weekends, she would fly home to spend time with him before coming back to the island to lead the team that were doing the interviews for the large number of resort staff that needed to be hired and trained. Along with that, she was still the main person who kept up with his meeting and travel schedule. He offered to let her bring someone else on board to do it, but like him, she didn't trust anyone but herself to handle his personal business. He told her anytime she felt overwhelmed, she had his permission to get more help as she needed it.

When he left the resort to fly home a week ago in order to help Tellum with anything he needed for wedding preparations, he thought about her and the way she smiled at him when he headed out to the airport. He'd stopped by the office for one last check of his schedule. He wanted them on the same page. He said his goodbyes and as he walked out, she commented that she would see him at the wedding. He turned and saw a look in her eyes that he wondered about. Keiko may not know it but her eyes reflected deep feelings, even profound thoughts. They told many stories.

There was something in how they looked at each other that day that had him unable to sleep on his flight. He needed that few hours' nap after having back-to-back meetings the day before that went well into the night. Images of Keiko plagued his mind, shifting him off-kilter. He wanted her; there was no doubt about that. The idea of her sensually fulfilled him. He'd been here before. There had been another, years ago. He hadn't quite gotten over her even now. What he was feeling for Keiko was different but as desirous as it could be. This was a first for him after vowing his first love had crushed him to the point that he was never going to let another woman get that close to him ever again. He'd suffered quietly through a broken heart. There was a pull to Keiko that was the hardest fight in his life when it came to his heart.

"I see Keiko made it," Tellum leaned over and spoke.

Tellum bringing her up brought him into the present.

"Yeah. I was surprised you invited her. Not that it's a problem or anything. I didn't realize she and Cheyenne were that close."

"Don't ask me about it. I had nothing to do with the invite list outside of our family and my close friends. As for Keiko, that was all Cheyenne."

"Really?" Byrum questioned.

Tellum nodded and nudged Cheyenne to get her attention.

"Baby, Byrum has a question for you," he said, moving so that Cheyenne could lean over in Byrum's direction.

"You finished dancing? I saw you tearing something up out there. The women are still wondering if you'll be returning to delight them with your moves. You have a question for me?"

Byrum winked at his new sister-in-law. He rolled his eyes at Tellum knowing that the competition between the three of them, including their brother Callum, had been about who the best dancer was. They all knew it was him who had the moves. Cheyenne just confirmed that. No doubt, Tellum was questioning the idea.

"Not really. I was just chatting with your husband."

"Oh, I love the sound of that. *My HUSBAND!*

Tellum leaned over and kissed Cheyenne. Byrum waved them off.

"Get a room!" he declared.

"Oh, we will! If this party doesn't soon wrap up, y'all are about to be short one bride and one groom," Tellum exclaimed. "What was it about Keiko that you wanted to ask Cheyenne?"

"Byrum?" Cheyenne questioned.

"Right. I was telling your husband that I was surprised that Keiko was invited. Not that there is anything wrong with that since I know the two of you are friendly with each other. I was just wondering. I didn't see anyone else from my team here, though I see Tellum's entire staff."

"I won't keep you in suspense, brother-in-law. I received a special request to add her to the guest list."

Byrum perked up. He wondered who would make such a request.

"Who did that come from?" he asked.

"Your mother. My mother, your mother and I had our first meeting about the guest list months ago. After your mother confirmed I had everyone from your family, she wrote down Keiko's name and asked if I was okay with that. I didn't question it for one minute. Was that, okay? Is something wrong?"

Byrum didn't bother looking around to catch his mother's eye. He loved her but he felt like she had something up her s

"Oh, no – nothing is wrong."

"She looks amazing right? I cannot believe she's not a model. I asked her about that earlier when we were on the dance floor. She said she gets that question all the time. She's more beautiful than the prettiest model out there. She has the killer looks that talent scouts are looking for," Cheyenne said.

Byrum looked at Keiko as she stood from her table. He had tried talking to her when he had come across his parents when they were slipping out of the party but Keiko had been stopped by some guy who asked her to dance and she obliged him. That's when he decided to make his way back to his seat. He hoped he'd done a good job of tampering down his dislike of seeing Keiko enjoy herself in another man's arms. He was so used to seeing her in work mode that her having any kind of personal life never entered his mind; at least not until the reality of his desire for her surfaced. He finally stopped pushing it to the side.

His eyes stayed on Keiko this time as she gave hugs all around to Tellum's staff who sat at the same table. He knew he shouldn't, but he wanted to talk to her. He wanted to dance with her earlier, but he pushed that thought out of his head. He didn't want any gossip. Keiko was at the wedding without a guest and so was he. It's true that the women tried to sidle up to him, but he could only think of Keiko and the gorgeous mint green dress with gold accessories to set the look up right that she confidently moved about in. There wasn't an eye in the place of any man that didn't have a lust-filled look when they saw her. He assumed that for the next few days, she would be spending time with her son. If he was going to talk with her, he needed to do it now. He was way from work. They were far away from his team who were back at Silent Whisper, the Blackstone brothers second newest resort located on a private island in the Mediterranean. He didn't lack confidence, but he did question his intention. He wanted her, but to what extent he could have her was up to her.

"Are you good if I head out?" he asked Tellum.

"Yeah. Things are winding down a bit. Cheyenne and I are going to say our goodnights in the next ten minutes or so. Make your escape if you need to. You staying here at the hotel tonight?"

"I am. I wasn't sure how late we would be. I know the fellas are trying to hang after, but I could use a quiet night. The days and nights have been long at the resort. This is the first real break I'm getting in weeks. I'm booked here for tonight with a late checkout tomorrow. I'm then headed to the condo for another day of being at home. As much as I miss my home here in Detroit, I'm also ready to get back to the resort. When do you and Cheyenne fly out to the Amalfi Coast?"

"We're here in the Presidential Suite for the next two nights. When we checkout, we head straight for the airport. Two amazing weeks of loving on my wife. I love the sound that makes coming out of my mouth. We'll talk when I get back?" Tellum asked.

"Yes. Don't even think of doing anything work related while you're gone. I've already told every member of your team that I'm firing anyone who reaches out to you or takes a call, text or email from you. I mean it, Tell. Not one iota of work."

"You don't have to worry about that. I told him unless there is some kind of family or medical emergency, there is to be no communication for any other reason to the outside world. I plan to keep him too busy to be able to focus on work," Cheyenne laughed and winked at Tellum.

"You heard her. The wife is in charge," Tellum boasted.

"Cool. I'm out. Looks like the fellas are all on the floor. I'll holler at them tomorrow. Tonight, I'm heading to peace and quiet."

Byrum stood from the table. His eyes caught up with Keiko as she left out of the doors at the back of the room. He had to rush to keep up with her. Instead of going through the crowd and risking someone stopping him, he exited out of the side door and raced toward the elevator. He wasn't sure if she was staying the night at the hotel or not. If so, there were only two banks of elevators that went to the wing of rooms for their guests.

Rushing with hurried steps, he caught a glimpse of her green dress as she rounded a corner. He caught up with her before she reached the elevators.

"Leaving so soon?" he asked when he reached her.

"Oh, hey! My feet are killing me in these heels. I don't know what I was thinking wearing these. They look good but aren't good for my feet long-term. I have more comfortable shoes in my room that I should have brought down with me."

"Maybe it's not the shoes. It may be all that dancing. Every time you sat down, a new suitor reached out for a dance. Did you turn anyone down?"

"I love to dance. Besides, the band was great. They played all the hits. Then the DJ wowed us, and I couldn't resist. Are you leaving?" she asked.

"I'm hoping to catch up on some much-needed rest while I'm home. I don't know when I'll get home again with all that's going on at the resort."

"Your schedule has been hectic. Let me know if you want me to reschedule anything once you return. You work too hard."

Byrum nodded and placed his hands in his pockets. He looked all around except for directly at her during the silence that lived between them.

"I do. I have to work on remedying that. Can I walk you to your room? I saw you and didn't have a chance to even say hello during the wedding or reception. Looks like we're headed in the same direction."

"Sure; that would be nice. You look nice in your black tuxedo and blue accents. The large wedding party looked fantastic. Did I see a photographer from *Essence Magazine*?"

she asked.

"You did. I asked Tellum about that. The magazine inquired about doing a spread and article on their wedding. He agreed as long as Cheyenne was okay with it."

"I can't wait to see that issue."

The elevator door opened, and they got in.

"You look amazing in green. You are killing everything in that dress. I hope that's okay to say," Byrum said.

He wanted to say more but held back.

"Yes, it is and thank you."

Then it happened; they rode in silence to the eighth floor. Byrum kept his eye on the elevator number above the door as if it was the most interesting thing in the world. He was nervous. Who was he? Women didn't make him nervous. Keiko was no ordinary woman. She was the object of his desire; a desire that was growing by leaps and bounds every day. Before long, the door opened and he followed her out. He strolled with her with his hands in his pockets. He needed to keep them there in the safe zone.

"This hotel is nice. I've never seen the inside of it this way. I've been to a few events in the ballroom. I'm usually in and out, going home. Like everyone else, I figured I wouldn't feel like doing that tonight."

"It's very nice. This is my first time here. My room is amazing, all white and crisp everything. Well, this is me," Keiko alerted him and pointed to her door.

She turned to face him, and they stood, again, in silence. The gaze between them tore through his heart. What could he say at this moment? His mind raced with a lot, but nothing seemed appropriate considering their work relationship. He had so much he wanted to pour out to her but didn't. He shifted on his feet. For a split second, he felt like there was something Keiko wanted to say, but like him, she was holding something back. He saw it in her eyes.

"Well, I hope you enjoyed yourself. It was nice seeing you in an arena outside of work," he finally said.

"I guess we never really have before without the entire team being around. I'm glad I came for the wedding. Cheyenne was beautiful. Everything was amazing. Again, you wear a tuxedo well," she beamed.

"Thank you. I like to play dress up every now and then when I'm not at one construction site or another."

"I guess I better go in."

Keiko turned her back to him and searched for her room key. Once she found it, she placed it in the door and it opened. She walked inside slowly, turning to him with the door in her hand.

Byrum opened his mouth to say what was on his mind and then stopped. He repeated that action and stopped again.

"Okay," was all he could get out.

"Is there anything else? You look like you want to say something?" she asked.

Byrum let his shoulders sink. Now wasn't the time. Perhaps never was more like it.

"No, I'm good. I guess I'll see you when I get back. Have fun with Tru. I know he can't wait to see you."

"My parents are flying in tomorrow evening from Boston. When I pick them up at the airport, we're going to pick Tru up for the next few days. I'm excited. Okay, then I'll see you when you get back the day after me, right?"

"I don't even know. That's something the best executive assistant knows for sure. I have to check my calendar."

"I'll text a reminder to you tomorrow."

"Don't you dare. I'll figure it out. Have a good night, Keiko."

"You too, Byrum."

She looked down and closed the door leaving him standing there alone. His eyes stayed on the door for what seemed forever before he turned and walked back down the hall, kicking himself for a missed opportunity. Now it was too late; or was it.

1

Byrum Blackstone stepped out of the glass-enclosed hotel shower after first a steely cold, then a piping hot shower. His mind had been on the incredibly gorgeous Keiko Lee, his executive assistant when the shower first began. He needed the chill of the cascading water to cool his overheated thoughts and body down. Why he couldn't shake his desire for her, he didn't know. He wished that he could. Life would be much easier for him if he did. She is why he had no interest in any other woman at this point in his life. When he imagined himself buried deep inside of a woman, it was her. He considered himself a lost cause now. He no longer lied to himself that Keiko wasn't under his skin, in his thoughts and making his body harden at the slightest thought of her.

Knowing it was deeper than that, his mind raced with thoughts of unending days and nights of having her in his arms. He kicked himself knowing his feelings were way deeper than casual sex, his usual approach to women and relationships. Keiko had him wondering what more with a woman would be like again. Heartbreak had him distancing his heart from anything other than mutual physical pleasure. Finally seeing Keiko for who she was beyond working for him had his heart getting involved in life once again. She was that amazing.

After drying off, he walked naked into the adjoined suite's bedroom and slipped on a pair of gray sweat pants and a plain white t-shirt. In bare feet, he walked out into the main area of his two-bedroom hotel suite, found the television remote and turned on the television to see what was streaming that could hold his attention. He looked in the black and gray backpack that he usually carried with him everywhere and pulled out the latest novel by one of his favorite crime story writers. Tossing the book to the long beige sofa, he went into the kitchen area and grabbed a bottle of water from the beverage center that sat under the long gray and white counter. He'd had enough to drink in the form of alcohol at his brother, Tellum and his new bride, Cheyenne's wedding reception. He needed to wind down, not have alcohol wind him back up.

Reaching for his phone that he'd left on the counter when he first arrived back to his hotel room, he checked for any texts or voice messages that could be important. This was the first time that he'd actually stepped away from work for more than a day or two. He needed this time off. What he didn't need was his every thought to be taken over by Keiko. It wasn't her fault for being so flawlessly beautiful. His eyes stayed on the screen of his phone hoping that an unexpected text would show up from her. He couldn't believe he left things unopened when it came to leaving her hotel room without telling her what was really on his mind.

Disappointment hit him like a punch to the gut. He only had himself to blame. He let the perfect moment to talk to her escape him when he let her close her hotel room door without saying what was on the tip of his tongue. His mind was too busy thinking about how delectable it would be to have his tongue wrapped around hers while he loved on her perfectly puckered lips. That thought was currently on his mind again.

Taking a big gup of the water, he moved to the sofa and channel searched. His laptop in his briefcase was calling his name. He had vowed to relax now that he was back home in Detroit and not on *Silent Whisper*, the resort he was anxious to get back to. Not letting temptation to work get to him, he placed his feet up on the table in front of him, crossing his legs at the ankles in an attempt to relax. He leaned back took in the quiet of the night. Usually, when he was back in Detroit, he would surf through his phone for company to help him release the tension in his life, especially in his body. Detroit was home, but his actual home is not where he played. He preferred to keep women from getting too close. Therefore, for fun, he spent time with them at one of his favorite five-star hotels. He was woman-less and workless tonight. It wasn't too often he could find himself in this position with nothing he needed to do that was related to work.

Though he was in town only for a brief moment, he looked through the calendar on his phone to make sure there was time in his schedule over the next day or so to stop in at the Blackstone Real Estate Investment Trust Corporation, the company he and his younger brothers, Tellum and Callum owned and ran together. They were masters at specializing in acquiring and developing luxury resorts around the world. They currently focused on resort management, branding and marketing and franchise licensing. They currently owned a Miami, Florida resort, one in Denver, Colorado and their most recent opening of *Secret Whisper* in Punta Cana was the largest, greatest and most popular resort so far. With the upcoming opening of *Silent Whisper* on a private island in the Mediterranean, he was sure it would be an even bigger and more epic launch than *Secret Whisper*.

Each of the brothers had taken on leading the development of each of their newest resorts. Tellum had led the effort at *Secret Whisper*. Byrum loved that he was leading the development of *Silent Whisper*. He marveled at his luck in being able to acquire the resort that could use a major overhaul.

He had been a frequent visitor at the old resort that had been on the island before he and his brothers bought it from the previous owner, a billionaire out of Dubai named Khalifa Mohamed. After Khalifa's wife died, leaving him to raise five children, he decided he no longer had an interest in owning and running the resort while living a long-distance life from his family who had remained in Dubai. He would travel home often and his family would make frequent trips to the island to visit him whenever he was there to check in on things.

Byrum had struck up a great friendship with Khalifa. When he was interested in selling, he gave the Blackstone's the first chance at acquiring it. They leaped at the chance on the location. Byrum quickly sold the idea to Tellum and Callum. It was easy to do and speak on since they knew how much he loved the Mediterranean side of the world.

Callum was taking responsibility for the last of their three new resorts, *Quiet Whisper*. This one would be located on a large portion of land they acquired in Hawaii. Like Silent Whisper, the resort in Hawaii already had a standing structure. With the acquisition of thousands of acres around it, they were looking to improve the current resort while also expanding on it. This location was special to them all. Their mother, Felicia, had grown up on the island. They still had a lot of family there. The same way in which he traveled to the

Mediterranean, Callum loved spending time in Hawaii where he also owned a three-bedroom condo.

Being the eldest at thirty-seven, his brothers often followed his guidance. When he told Callum to stop spending all of his money on hotels or staying with family, where he didn't want to be anyway, he convinced him that instead of all of that, he should buy a small place now that they could afford it. Callum reached out to their favorite travel agent and had done just that. Their family had a larger vacation home in Hawaii, but Callum felt it was too large for him to maintain on his own. Callum's place made him happy. That was all that mattered.

Tellum's place in Detroit was the biggest and most magnificent condo he'd ever seen. His own unit was more than one floor and sat at the top of a five-level building with a small number of tenants. He and Cheyenne were planning to make that their permanent home for a few years.

Byrum loved that he and his brothers were close. They had their battles, but nothing could come between the love they had for each other. Because of that, they were able to build an empire that continued to spur new ideas, new business ventures and great capital. Speaking of Callum, he hadn't had the chance to talk to his brother much over the past few days while they were all in town for the wedding.

Flipping through the television channels, Byrum contemplated ignoring his ringing cell phone until he saw who was calling.

"Callum! What's up brother? I was just thinking about you because we haven't had much time to connect since I arrived. I don't think we've had a lot of time to chat at all these past few weeks," Byrum noted.

"Hey, bro. That's true. We did have a good time at Tellum's bachelor party at *Secret Whisper*. That there was a time and a half!" Callum cheered.

"Now, you know what happened on the island, stays on the island, right? Neither one of us would ever have disrespected Cheyenne with any untoward things occurring but having thirty-five men join us on the island for a weekend of havoc was a good time."

"I don't think I've ever seen so much food and drinks get devoured in one night. Hey, it's not every day that our brother gets married. I never knew Tellum's professional football player friends could eat so much!"

Byrum nodded his agreement as if Callum could see him. He closed his eyes and thought back to a few weeks ago on the island. Fun was an understatement.

"Cheyenne knew her new brothers wouldn't do anything too outlandish."

"I looked around at the reception before I left and realized I hadn't seen you for at least thirty minutes. Tellum said you'd left to go to your room early. You good?" Callum asked.

"Yeah, I'm good. It's been a wild couple of days. I flew in from *Silent Whisper* after a week of getting back there from Denver. I needed some down time. I figured I'd put in enough time today. I checked to be sure Tellum was good with me heading out early. Besides, he didn't question when mom and dad slipped out."

Callum laughed on the other end of the phone.

"I checked that too. Where did they go? Dad wanted to get home early for a business trip or something? I thought he changed that meeting in Los Angeles so that I could go with him. I promised a friend I'd attend his listening party for his upcoming rap album and then I would be free."

"He told me about that and said he had delayed the travel plans. Bro, you do not want to know what he and mom slipped away to do. Now, Pop didn't say the actual words but I saw it on his face. Mom looked shyly away. Pop, still go it!" Byrum yelled.

"Eww – now I can't get that out of my head. I just hope when you and I find our perfect women and get married, we still love on our wives like Pop does with mom all the time. They think we don't see how he looks at her."

"Man, don't put any images in my head either. As for marriage, I'm going to leave that up to you and Tell. I'm *never* getting married. After getting as close to doing that as I did, only to be slapped in the face with reality, I'm not doing that ever again. Women need to settle for me being and staying single. I will happily die up on this bachelor hill."

Byrum made it clear to everyone around him that there would be no marriage for him. He would never let a woman get into his heart the way his ex-girlfriend did. She was a stone's throw and a big ass diamond ring away from being his fiancé until she wasn't.

"How long are you going to let what Valencia Gastaud did keep that heart of yours on ice? What she did was *foul*," Callum expressed. "It was dirty. She didn't deserve you or your love. That doesn't mean another woman doesn't. Speaking of Valencia, do you ever hear from her? I saw a social media article about her husband having some outside baby or something."

Byrum had seen that story along with a few others. It seems her decision to leave him wasn't a good one. He didn't know how much truth there was to it since they no longer stayed in contact. He was still pissed off enough to want to say that if it was true, she deserves it, but he didn't. He let the idea go out of his head. He didn't want anything about Valencia to live in his head anymore just like he removed traces of her from his heart.

"Naw, I haven't talked to her, though I know she's called the office a few times and sent a couple of emails. I haven't responded."

"Are you going to?"

"Hell no! You know what that woman did to me. I had just left the jewelry store from picking up what was to be her engagement ring. On my flight to Monaco to visit her and to talk to her father about marrying her, I get a call from Tellum that he heard she was engaged to some Prince who was also from Monaco. I thought it was gossip for social media. It wasn't until I got that dreadful call from her telling me that we couldn't see each other anymore. Her father picked out someone he expected her to marry in a few days. He needed to close a business deal and Valencia allowed herself to be the pawn in that game. Who allows themselves to be, pretty much, sold to the highest bidder in this day and age? She knows that I'm the last person she should ever reach out to a year later. I don't know why she has. I'm not interested in anything she has to say. I understand that she and some friends were recently at our Miami resort. She spent so much time asking about me that a member of our team called to let me know in case I wanted to reach out to her. I didn't and I let that go."

"What did you do with the ring?" Callum asked.

Byrum thought about the platinum diamond ring. He hadn't held on to it long.

"After I had the pilot file a new flight plan in order to turn us around, I went back to the jewelry store the next day and returned it. Even though the jeweler was willing to give me all of the money back, I let him keep half of the cost for himself. I didn't want him to completely lose out on the sale to me. That was my first and last time buying an engagement ring. No more ideas of marriage for me. As for you, I see that just like I saw it for Tellum. I knew the minute he'd met Cheyenne that they would get married. Even though her father worked against them and us because our dad wouldn't help him in a business deal, Cheyenne eventually realized that, unlike Valencia, her heart wasn't for sale to anyone. She wanted and needed to love only Tellum. Only he could make her happy. She's perfect."

"You don't think there is a perfect woman out here for you? Not even Keiko?" Callum asked.

Hearing him mention her name, Byrum uncrossed his legs and leaned forward.

"Really, Callum?"

"Don't shoot daggers at me. I feel them coming. Tell told me you left when Keiko left. He said you followed her out to talk to her. Did you?"

Leaning back, Byrum exhaled a loud breath of frustration at himself. Hopefully, his pursuit of Keiko wasn't obvious to anyone else.

"No, I didn't. For the first time in my life, a woman makes me nervous. That's how I am around her. I know it's crazy. It's pure lust. She's so freaking sexy. Those long, beautiful legs? *Man!*"

"Does Tellum know about your desire for Keiko or am I still the only person you've told?"

"Only you. I can't risk what might happen. I told you about

that. Tellum may suspect. His behavior tonight is making me think that. I questioned Keiko being invited to the wedding. I thought it was odd. Tellum tried to make a big thing about it."

"Byrum, you are worried about what others would say if you hooked up with her and someone found out. So what? She's a grown ass woman just like you are. Sure, she works directly for you. You and Keiko would not be the first people in the history of the business world to want to slip and slide around in the sheets together though you're boss and employee. It's not a crime if you're in it together."

"For starters, I don't even know if she's interested in me in that way."

"Oh, please. After you told me about her, every time I see her, I can see how she looks at you. You and I can both read women well. She wants to see and experience what's under those expensive suits. She's gorgeous. She has eyes for you too."

"That may be the case, but she deserves so much more than a man who is only interested in getting between her legs. I'm not trying to sound crass, but as sexy as she is, there isn't a man who hasn't thought that about her. What can I say, I'm all man and I love sexy women."

Byrum leaned back, closed his eyes and try to understand how he got here. Millions of women in the world and she's who he can't stop thinking about; the woman who works for him.

"Bro, there is more to it than that with her, but I'll let it go. Your bed is never, ever cold. We are Blackstone men. It's what we do. We're not shy about our lust for women and getting our taste of them. As long as we're clear with them what our intentions are, there is no need to be sorry about our purpose. Women don't turn you down for sex simply because you may want a one-night stand or a friend-with-benefits situation. Perhaps Keiko is looking for that kind of relationship. You told me that her divorce was contentious. Sounds to me like she isn't looking for anything more at this time in her life. Do you know if she's dating anyone? Have you seen her with anyone on the island?"

Byrum tried to recall and couldn't think of an instance of seeing her with anyone other than staff. No one after hours other than her friends.

"Not that I know of, but that doesn't mean anything. Her ex-husband did a number on her. She told me once that their relationship had been great when they dated. After they got married, he stopped treating her like an equal and more like property. She didn't really pick up on it until after she was already pregnant with her son. Some years later, she couldn't take it anymore. I understand there were some really bad times. Luckily, it sounds like they have worked out an arrangement to get along for the sake of their son. He lives here in Detroit with his father while she's on the island helping to get the resort up and running. I think she's planning on returning to the main office here in Detroit in a few months when the new staff are hired and in place. Like me, she's focused on work, I think. I haven't seen her have much of a life other than hanging out with her friends around the island."

"You had a chance to talk to her tonight and you didn't do it?"

"I could have. I'm usually a man of many words. Around her, I don't want to say the wrong thing. I'm her boss, Cal. I can't just approach her with an offer of the best sex I think she and I could have together. There has to be some kind of sexual harassment thing that could come to fruition there. I like her as my assistant. She knows me better than I know myself. She finishes my thoughts and my sentences. She's perfect. I question myself about ruining that."

"Listen to yourself. She's perfect. She knows you. She finishes your sentences. She's not just perfect; she's perfect for *you*, Byrum. Look, all I know is, nothing hurts more than a try that never happens. No one has to know. If you approach her right, letting her know that you like her and that what you feel is far from what the working relationship is, she is either okay with it or she isn't. I don't think it will impact your ability to still work together. You'll never know if you don't go for it. You're always the one giving me and Tell advice on everything in our lives. You introduced me to Kendra through one of your WNBA coach friends. We listen. I'm listening to you right now and I'm not judging. I also don't want you to miss out on the perfect woman. I know you say it's lust and about sex, but I know you – it's more than that. When you realize it too, let me know. It's a shame that you and her are far away from work on the island, in the same hotel and in private rooms. There are no eyes on you. Think about that. I'm in my car headed home. Call me before you fly out. Let's have drinks before then even if it's at the airport. I'll be at *Silent Whisper* in a few weeks. We can also connect in person then."

"I hear you and I appreciate you. I'll think about it. Get home safe. I'll holler at you tomorrow."

After the call ended, Byrum turned off the television as if it was impeding his ability to think. Could his brother be right? Is he thinking too hard about this? Did he miss an opportunity to at least talk to Keiko without having eyes from the island on them? He looked at the time and it was still pretty early; not quite nine. For him, this was early. He wondered if Keiko was already in bed. Tomorrow, she would be gone to spend time with her son. After that, the next time he would see her would be back on the island. Callum was right. It was now or never to talk to her. He wouldn't get much rest if he didn't.

Going into the bedroom, he grabbed his favorite pair of Nike's. As soon as he cut the bedroom light off, he stopped in the doorway. His mind went to where he didn't want it to go. He was filled with a bunch of, what ifs. He couldn't chance not being ready. He grabbed one additional item he needed, grabbed his phone from the sofa and left his suite. It was now or not at all.

2

"This dress is everything, Madison. Thanks for helping me pick it out. The red one would have been too much."

Keiko turned her head to the left and then to the right, taking in the emerald green dress from every angle. Placing it on a hanger, she placed it in her overnight bag. It wasn't often that she got the chance to dress up like she did for Cheyenne and Tellum's wedding and reception earlier. She loved being sexy. She grew up enjoying playing with dolls and dressing them up in evening gowns. She and her best friend, Madison Albright, had similar childhood stories about dolls, dressing them up and dreaming about their own weddings one day. They talked about it a lot after they met when they ended up living across the hall from each other in her first apartment after college.

After graduating from the University of Detroit Mercy with her undergraduate degree in Business Management, she had decided to stay in the town she loved so much after interviewing for her first job at a Fortune 500 company in Detroit. That's where she'd gotten her start in the working world. It was also the place where she'd met her ex-husband, DeConnor Brooks.

After a year's long relationship, they were engaged and married within a few months. That's when life had been good.

Things didn't end that way. They were now divorced. She was still dealing with the result of the bumpy road to the end. She left the company to get away from DeConnor. That was when she interviewed for the job with Byrum Blackstone. She never looked back. Working for him and his brothers was the best job she'd ever had.

"I told you that dress was made for you. I'm glad you trusted me to pick it out for you. Coming back to Detroit two days before the wedding made for good timing to make sure the dress fit. I've never seen a woman with a body that was created for a dress like you. What am I saying, that body of yours is perfect in everything. Did you wear your hair up or down?"

Keiko zipped up the dress bag and placed it back in the closet. She would take it back to the apartment that she moved into after her divorce. Because of her son, Tru, the judge in their divorce had asked her if she wanted to keep the home that she and DeConnor had bought together. Keiko declined because she wanted a new start. Besides, the five-bedroom, four-bathroom house was too big for her and Tru. At one point in her marriage, she and DeConnor were planning on having several children. Instead, she moved into a three-bedroom, three bath apartment that she loved. There was plenty of space for her and Tru. At five years old, he had more toys than any little boy should have. Spoiling him was what gave her great joy. He was a good little boy.

She turned and walked over to the mirror where she ran her hands through her long, thick black hair, making sure it was dry before she put the hotel-provided hair dryer back in the closet.

"I wore it down. I tried up and didn't care for it. I think

I'm going to cut it. I have enjoyed having it long and flowing down my back. I want more freedom. I'm thinking of getting it cut right at my shoulders. What do you think?"

"Go for it! You mentioned that before. I told you then that it was a good idea. Do what you want. So many decisions you made or didn't make were because of what DeConnor thought. He no longer has a say. Take your freedom seriously and do what you want. The answer is, cut it and keep it moving. It's going to be sexy. You'll go from long and thick hair to short and thick; still as sexy. Besides, does Byrum like women with longer or short hair?"

Keiko stopped moving. Her hand stayed in her hair. She looked down at her cellphone where it sat with the speaker on, resting on top of the wedding program that she'd yet to put away in her luggage.

"Here *you* go!" Keiko leaned over the dresser and said directly into the phone. Her elbows rocked nervously on the redwood dresser.

"That man is some kind of gorgeous. If I was in a position to move to an island, I would beg you to get me a job so that I can look at him every single day. I mean, I wouldn't because I know you have the hots for him. The rule of thumb is, we do not go after our best friends' men. I'm just saying, he is fine girl. You are right to lust after him like you do. He still doesn't know? How did he look at the wedding? Was he fine as hell in a tuxedo? Did his bowlegs wow you? My inquiring mind needs to know!" Madison hollered into the phone.

Keiko reached inside of her suitcase and pulled out a red silk nightie with matching panties and slipped both on over her nakedness. She grabbed the matching robe and tied the thin strap around her waist. Even though she was alone, she still enjoyed sexy things on her body; especially soft, satiny lingerie. Her plan for the night was to relax and listen to some music. She seldom got the chance to do that. Now with talk of Byrum, she was flustered. Her body sizzled ardently with images in her head of him. She was remembering a recent sighting of him in the office after he stopped by from the gym before going home. He was all sweaty with his powerful thighs making every woman who saw him swoon. She was a part of that number. Just the thought of the man did sexy things to. Then she remembers that Byrum is her boss and she refocuses her mind on what she was going to have for lunch; she needed that distraction.

She moved to the bed, placed the phone on it so that she could finish adding lotion to her legs. The rest of her body she'd done right after her hot shower. It should have been a cold one since Byrum had been on her mind the entire time. In her head, with her eyes closed, it was his hands that were spreading the soapy suds across her body in all of her sexy, sensitive places. That wasn't the first time he was the star of one of her showers. She knew it wouldn't be the last.

"You ask too many questions. For starters, yes, he looked damn good in a tuxedo. But then, I'm biased because he looks good in everything I've ever seen him in. No, he doesn't know that I would like to tear his clothes off of him and ride him until the sun came up every day."

Keiko giggled to herself. She was more blunt these days and she loved it.

"Girlllllll! I can't believe this is you I'm hearing this from. You were so closed up about what you want and desire because of DeConnor. I still cannot believe that the intimacy you shared was all about his needs. You didn't say anything about that. Why, I still don't get, but you're free from that prison that was your marriage. I thought that you would never want to be close to a man again. Since the divorce, I have never heard you say anything about a man like you do about Byrum."

"He's my boss! I feel shameful for even thinking it."

"Why? Who cares that he's your boss. If you like and want him, that's what you should do. What's stopping you? From what we have talked about, he's not shy about silently telling you how much he desires you. It's in those eyes and that babyface. You said people call him that?"

"Yes. He's the oldest brother at thirty-seven but he's the youngest looking. In fact, people think he's in his twenties. He gets that from his mother. She still looks like she's in her forties. Callum and Tellum, who are just as good looking, take their looks from their father. He's darker and their mother is lighter like Byrum. Some days, it's hard working around Byrum. I have often rushed home to get to my toy collection. I see what other women say when they think I'm not listening; especially around the office."

"Has he ever been with anyone around the office that you know of?"

"No. The executive team was out with him when we first arrived on the island. The topic came up about interoffice relationships and how he felt about that. He didn't care. He only said it wasn't for him. On the island, we all know each other but have not really ventured out to meet any of the people who live on the island all year. I know when people think about it, they think of it as a small, secluded island, but it's not. It's as large as the Dominican Republic. Our small area is the size of Punta Cana. It's not tiny. There are schools, businesses, colleges, malls, amusement parks, zoos and everything else just like places like that and Jamaica or Bermuda. For now, we've been staying pretty close. Byrum said that he believes people are adult and mature enough who work for him to know what is and isn't allowed or tolerated. He likes to let people decide for themselves as long as there is no level of harassment. He believes that where people find intimacy, love and romance is up to them and their hearts."

"Okay! I like that way of thinking. That means that if you want him, you should go for him but don't pinch his butt or nothing like that. I mean, unless you're with him in a shower or something and then all bets are off. You should pinch away," Madison laughed.

Keiko laughed out loud with her.

"If I had that man in a shower with me, I'm pinching everything, touching everything, sucking...oops, did I say that out loud?"

Keiko couldn't stop the cackling laugh that escaped her lips after almost saying the word.

"Dirty mouth. Go wash it out with soap!" Madison joked. "Seriously though, if you find that he is interested in devouring every part of you, are you going to say no?"

"I've lusted after him for a long time. It has taken everything in me to not be the aggressive one. I don't know how to be that. DeConnor never let me."

Keiko let the thought live in the air. Her life with her ex-husband was still pretty painful to think about. She felt like a Stepford wife, based on an old movie she liked to watch. Madison was the only person who knew what she'd gone through. Byrum knew some stuff because he was supportive as she was going through her divorce. The fact that her body is on fire every time she's in Byrum's presence was a testament to the new woman she had become. No other man has ever made her feel as desired as he does, even if he didn't know it.

"Don't let that lust sleep. Let it out. Let it live in and around you. There is nothing wrong with wanting a man the way you want Byrum, boss or not. You read those sexy, steamy romance novels about bosses and their assistants burning up the sheets. They live happily ever after. That could be you and Byrum, you never know."

Keiko thought about that and her body sagged against the headboard of the bed. As she rubbed the last bit of lotion into her leg, she couldn't forget that Byrum had been hurt by a woman before. It was the same woman who recently started calling the office trying to connect with him. From that failed relationship came a lot of heartache for him. It ran so deep that he proudly professed that he would never fall for another woman. She'd seen him date, or what he called date but was really headboard banging friends. She got that terminology from one of her friends. Not one of those women made him reconsider his take on being in a relationship. She hated that for him because even if she wasn't the woman for him, she hoped someone would be. He would make a great boyfriend and one day, husband.

Byrum loved people hard. He has the biggest heart of any person she's ever met. He was wasting it by not letting his heart be open to more than sex with a woman. At this point in her life, she wanted him so much, she would settle for a hot romp in the bed; in the shower, on the floor. She didn't care where it was. She had an itch for him that she knew would never go away until only he scratched it.

"It won't be. He's had the worst kind of hurt from a

relationship that I won't go into. Let me just say that if any woman thinks she's going to tame and lock Byrum into anything more than being a bed buddy, she can forget it. He's about his business, his wealth and as often as he can, getting a sexual release from sexy, hot women. That man loves a gorgeous woman."

"You think you're not one of those women? You are selling yourself short. You are *Miss Exotic.* Those dab and drab clothes DeConnor had you wearing didn't do you or all that sexiness you walk around wither everyday any justice. You are a butterfly now, honey. Fly, fly and then fly some more. Take life by the neck and wring it until what you want and who you want to be falls out."

Keiko thought of Byrum and fanned herself.

"Whew! The things the idea of him do to me. I'm scared. We have a great working relationship. I love my job. The pay is incredible. As his assistant, I get a housing allowance along with my regular large pay check. They pay my travel cost, of course for business, but I'm also entitled to a stipend for personal travel. I still had some of it left to cover my stay here or I would have stayed with you so that we could hang out while I'm subletting my apartment for a few weeks to my cousin who's here while her place is being upgraded. Look, I can't lose this job because I'm lusting after my boss. It's inappropriate."

"No, it isn't. Stop saying that. You found a man that you want to enjoy. I think he is thinking the same thing but neither of you are saying it."

Keiko nibbled on her bottom lip before she spoke to reveal what happened an hour ago.

"Tonight, he chased me down when I was walking back to

my room. He walked me all the way to the door. His eyes were so smoldering. I know because his eyes are a light brown color, which is rare for a Black man. Again, he gets that from his mother. When he looked at me, they turned black as coal. I don't see that often. I felt like he wanted to say something. Perhaps he even wanted to come in but the words never came."

"You didn't say anything?"

"I tried to drag out saying goodnight for as long as I could. I didn't know what else to say or do. I'm new at this. I haven't had an interest in a man since DeConnor. I haven't dated because I was taking time to find out who I was again. Now that I know who I am, I know what I want and it's him. Still, I'm nervous about it. What if we hook up and people find out? The talk about me would be brutal. I love my job, Madison."

"And you want that man. How did you leave it?"

"We said goodnight and I closed the door. I stood there for a few seconds to see if he would knock. I looked through the peep hole. He stood there for a few seconds and then he turned and walked down the hall to the elevator. He's in one of the top floor suites, I'm sure."

"Girl, if there was ever a missed opportunity, you just had one. Ugh, you make me so mad when you don't go for what you want. You have a chance to do that now and you still won't. You are letting what could be gossip around the office get to you. You know me – I would plant a hot sexy kiss on him in front of everyone and walk away with my head held high. It's a new day and age. Women are just as forward as men. Don't let him slip and slide into a woman that he will realize he can't live without. I know it's a long shot based on how you say he is about being involved, but I still believe that the woman for him is you. Think about that. I have to run. My niece is coming over to spend the night. My sister is going away on business in the morning. I'll have Shiloh for a few days. Her and my baby girl will have fun playing together. Call me before you leave to go back to the island. We should take all of the kids for ice cream."

"Tru would love that. You know he loves his godmother. You're the only person who spoils him more than me."

"I need to see my little man. I reached out to DeConnor a week ago about getting Tru for a night. Surprisingly, he said yes. I'm planning on getting him for the weekend during one of the times that you don't come home to be with him."

"You know he is going to love, love that. You go ahead and do what you need to do. I'm going to get comfy in this big ass bed that is definitely made for a queen. It's been a long day. I've never really stayed in a hotel in Detroit since I have a place. I love the idea and will definitely do it again."

"Do you have to check out early tomorrow?"

"No. I'm going to stay here for the rest of my time in town. Like I said, my cousin has taken over my place. Besides, I don't feel like entertaining her. She doesn't know I'm in town. I'm hoping to sleep in late. I'll leave when it's time to pick up my parents around three in the afternoon when their flight comes in. I'll call you so we can connect before I head back to the island."

"Sounds like a plan. Remember, don't let Byrum slip through your fingers. Even if he's looking for a friends-with-benefits only, I can't begin to tell you how much you will enjoy that. What you had with DeConnor was sex. It wasn't even good sex. You need someone to really put it on you to show you what you have been missing for years in that marriage. My vote is on Byrum."

Keiko waited before she answered. And then she did.

"Mine is too."

When the call ended, Keiko got up and put her toiletries away. She turned on the television and turned out the light. She was about to slip under the comforter when her phone rang again. She thought it was Madison forgetting to tell her something. Instead, her heart skipped a beat when Byrum's face showed up on the screen. She answered quickly.

"Hello?"

"Hi, Keiko. Am I disturbing you?" Byrum questioned.

"No, not at all. Is everything okay? Don't tell me you looked at your schedule and something is off."

Byrum laughed which caused her to laugh with him.

"Not at all. You are too precise for anything to be wrong. I was hoping I could talk to you for a few minutes about something personal and not work related. Are you okay with that?"

Keiko grabbed her lips between her teeth and held them while her head moved up and down. Then she remembered, she needed to answer.

"Um, yes, sure. Is something wrong?"

"Yes."

She didn't know what to say next. She couldn't read his one-word response. If she was in his presence, she would be able to tell if his answer was a good yes or a bad one. Over the phone, she couldn't tell.

"Okay. Is it something I can help with?" she offered.

Byrum didn't answer her. She could hear his ragged breathing on the other end and wondered what he was doing. He was breathing faster and faster.

"Okay, I'm going to say something and please, let me know if I'm being inappropriate and I'll never, ever do this again. We work great together. I don't want anything to change that. It's just that what I'm about to say could ruin that and it's the last thing I want."

"Byrum, you're scaring me."

"I'm sorry. That's not my intention at all. Okay – let me talk and get this out."

"Okay."

Keiko stood and paced around the carpeted bedroom floor. She was nervous. She braced herself for whatever he was about to share.

"Tonight, when I walked you to your room, I wanted to say something but fear of how it would be received kept me from saying it. Have you noticed anything different about me when I'm around you?"

"I have. It's in the way you look at me."

Keiko shocked herself at how easily her response rolled off of her lips.

"Does it make you uncomfortable?"

"Not at all."

"How does it make you feel?"

"Sexy."

Madison's words rang in her head. She wasn't going to hold back no matter what.

"And?"

"Desired."

"If I told you that I was hoping you would feel that way, would I be out of line? Please don't answer in a way that you think you should because it's me, the man you work for. I want you to give me an honest answer."

"No, Byrum. You would not be out of line. The way you make me feel is very much received and accepted. That's Keiko Lee, the woman talking, not the person who works for you."

"But there is that, isn't there? You work for me and to be as honest as I can, I do desire you. I think that you are the sexiest woman in the world. I've been attracted to you for a while now. I have struggled with what that means and what it could mean if I acted on it. I wanted to tell you that so badly tonight when I walked you to your room. I didn't want you to get the wrong idea that I was being forward because we're alone here at the hotel and away from prying eyes of the staff. I can honestly say that I don't know how to proceed here. I know what I want, but I also don't want to do anything to hurt you in any way. I didn't know how you felt or if you felt any kind of way about me. There is a lot that could be jeopardized. I'm only thinking about you. I don't want anything to happen that would make it awkward or hard for you around the office. I've never desired anyone around the office before; not even slightly. I wanted to tell you that tonight. Seeing you here at the wedding reminded me that I've been fighting this for so long that I don't seem to know how to do anything but want you. My desire for you overpowers my senses. How can I feel this way without crossing a line?"

Keiko felt for him. There was no way that this could be easy for him. She cared about him. If he was admitting all of this to her, it must have taken everything in him to do so. Her heart melted with each word.

"It's not crossing a line if I feel the same way; and trust me, I do. I was just talking about you to Madison. I was telling her how much I desire you, desire to be with you but I am also scared about what it could do to the working relationship. If anything happens and people find out, what could that mean? You know I met my ex-husband in an office setting. We didn't work together at all and it was totally different. This is new for me. None of my old bosses were even on my radar for anything. That's not to say that they didn't hit on me. I don't feel like that's what you're saying or doing. This is mutual. Let yourself off of the hook in thinking there is anything wrong or that there are any lines crossed."

"I wanted to kiss you so bad. I have for a long time. That's only the start. Like I said, I didn't want to hurt you. I didn't want to lead you on. I didn't want to take advantage of my position as your boss. I have been fighting my desire for you hard. I was in my room finally tired of fighting it. I felt like I may have had a chance if I had just talked to you when I was there earlier."

She was confused.

"Are you saying that the moment has passed? The chance is gone?"

"I don't want it to be. That's why I'm calling. I'm afraid to go to bed without telling you how I feel. I'm not sure I'd have the nerve once we're back at work. My feelings felt so wrong but also felt very right."

"I understand. Byrum, if I was any other woman that you desired like this, would you have asked to come into her hotel room tonight? Would you have hesitated to do so?"

"No, I wouldn't have hesitated. Not if I wanted her as much as I want you."

"But not me?"

"You're different. You're special. I know you. You know me and what I'm like when it comes to women. I don't offer them more than what happens in the bedroom. That's all I have. I see you as someone who would want and expect more. That could make for an uncomfortable environment."

"Not if I am the same way. My marriage and the divorce were hard on me. I lived a sheltered life for a long time. I'm interested in exploring a different side of me. If I say I'm interested in no strings attached for one night only, what would you say?"

Keiko waited through the pause. And then he spoke.

"I would say, come open the door. I'm on the other side."

3

Byrum had been holding his breath since Keiko disconnected their call. He was left with an uncomfortable level of uncertainly as he stood on the other side of the door. He looked up and down the hallway and didn't notice anyone moving about.

He felt plagued with anticipation of whether or not they were on the same page. Waiting for what seemed like an eternity, Byrum rocked from one foot to the other for any sound of the door being unlocked from the other side. After their talk, he didn't want to believe that she wouldn't come to the door. Every part of him wanted her. He was shocked that there wasn't a part of him that he was willing to hold back from his feelings. For a self-proclaimed bachelor whose heart he thought was unreachable, he chuckled at how badly he wanted to be on the other side of the door. Not just for the intimacy, but seriously, for the love he felt every time he was in her presence. Perhaps his brother was right. There was more to his desire for Keiko that was beyond the physical.

Putting his phone in the pocket of his sweatpants, his fingers touched on what he remembered to bring with him. He wondered if he should have been this optimistic. This was Keiko. He could see himself wanting and having more. Was she going to give him a chance to prove how compatible he secretly felt they were?

When he was about to give up, it happened.

He heard the sound that had him exhaling a heavy breath while patting his heart with his index and middle fingers.

Keiko was opening the door. Even if she didn't invite him in, he would get the chance to talk more and set his eyes on her beauty. He'd never met a woman who sent a lightning bolt shock to all of his senses the way she did every single day. Once he finally admitted that to himself, he thought of no other woman except her.

As the door opened slowly, Byrum kept his eyes level to where he knew he'd come eye-to-eye with Keiko the minute she opened the door. He thought he was prepared for what he would see and how he would feel. The minute he saw her eyes, all thought left his head and flew to other parts of his body.

"Damn."

"Huh?" Keiko questioned.

Byrum smiled, taking in everything about her from her long hair being down and cascading around her body to her face, then her chest and body covered in red satin and finally down to her feet with glittery toe nails. When his eyes traveled back up her body, they stopped at her full lips covered in a sheer sheen that seemed to be calling his name. He didn't answer; not yet. If given the chance, he would answer it until they needed to break apart from each other to breathe.

"I'm sorry. I shouldn't have said that but my brain stopped working when you opened the door. You look amazing. Believe me, the word damn was a compliment. I honestly couldn't think of anything else. When I boldly called you to tell you what I was thinking and feeling, I'm seeing so much through new eyes. If I say damn again, just know that the blood rushed out of my head to other, southern parts of me," he joked.

Keiko laughed and the mood lightened with an intensity that sparked a hot coupling of pining. He was remembering their conversation and hoping that the same sentiment they talked about out of each other's physical presence still held now that they stood together. There was an unfamiliar level of nervousness that kept him planted in place; unsure of whether he should move or not.

"It's okay. For as long as we have been working together, are you as brand-new at this moment like I'm feeling?" she asked.

"I think more me than you. It took me all day, actually longer than that, to get up the nerve to call you tonight. Are you glad I did?"

Keiko nodded and moved.

"Come in, Byrum. Let's not give anyone else who has a room on this floor a front row seat to you being here."

"Always protecting me," he said.

"I always will."

Byrum willed his legs to move.

"Right. That's a good idea."

He moved around her before turning in her direction while she closed the door behind him. His eyes quickly panned around. He looked down at his hands which felt moist from sweating. He rubbed them on his pants and waited for Keiko to turn around. She did so in what appeared to him to be slow motion. When her eyes landed on every spot around him but on him, he moved his head so that where her eyes traveled, he would be front and center. What he didn't want was for her to feel uncomfortable around him.

"Byrum, I don't know what to say here," she finally stuttered out.

"They way you say my name is enough for me. I have always loved how you say my name. It's like you say it with a whisper. I think as my attraction to you has grown, it sounds sexier coming from you than any other woman, ever. Thanks for inviting me in. Red is most definitely your color. I'm sorry if my stare is making you uncomfortable, but I just can't look away."

When Keiko tried to pull the red satin robe tighter around her body, he knew that she was, in fact, feeling awkward. He must have caught her preparing for bed. He was having his luckiest day ever.

"When you called, I was getting ready for bed after my shower. I was going to relax and listen to some music."

When her eyes darted about again after she moved her hair out of her face and back behind her shoulder, he knew he had to do something. They were standing here as if they weren't two adults who have been attracted to anyone before. He was trying to tread lightly.

"Keiko, look at me," he finally said.

Though he wanted to reach for her, he didn't. They were alone. There were no prying eyes. Even with that, he wanted her to be as comfortable around him as she always had been. The situation was different, sure. Seeing her relaxed around him in every setting was important. When she looked at him, he relaxed his shoulders and moved closer to where she stood with her back against the locked door. He made sure to leave room between them.

"I'm nervous," she admitted.

"So am I."

"No, Byrum. You are not a man who is ever nervous. I know you."

"You're right. You do know me. That Byrum you know very well. This one, standing here in front of you? I'm hoping you'll give me the chance to introduce you to him. That is, if you want to. I know we chatted on the phone about the implications. I want to reiterate how important it is to me that my first concern is how you feel about anything that may happen between us. We are in a strange position as boss and employee. I would never, ever cross a line that didn't make you feel welcoming about it."

She nodded, closed her eyes and then looked back up at him again.

"This is so new to me. Not just because it's you and me. I haven't been this close to a man with a bed in the room since I was married. I think it's because I had thoughts and dreams about you. I couldn't imagine anyone else. I tried not to have those thoughts. I swear I did. They were so inappropriate."

Byrum's radar went up and so did his left eyebrow.

"Oh? That is not a bad thing," he offered and fanned himself. They laughed together.

"They are if you're my boss."

"Okay, how about if you and I put that relationship on the side for now. We're here and we're alone. We're not on the island where the team is. No one knows I'm here with you right now. Well, Callum might know, but he and Tellum have always been the keeper of my secrets."

He was going to continue but the sight of Keiko's eyes widening after hearing him say Callum may know had him holding on to his next thought.

"Callum? What does Callum know?" she questioned.

"All cards on the table?" he asked.

"Yes. Every one of them. I will do the same."

"Keiko, it's so hard to think rationally with you looking like a goddess. I'll try my best."

When he winked at her, he was happy that she smiled. Her body also seemed to relax.

"Should we sit?" he asked.

"I can't. I can't move from this spot."

"Are you okay?"

"Byrum, I have never been the kind of woman who takes initiative or the first step with a man. When I opened the door and you were standing there looking all hot, rugged and all the things I think of when I see you, I could only see us over there on that bed. My mind is racing with all kinds of thoughts so, for now, can we stand here and get the words out? Callum?" she asked again.

Byrum got it. He was right with her.

"He is the one I talk to most of the time. My brothers and I share in deep conversations, especially about women. If you tell too many people, that's how rumors and gossip get out. I keep my thoughts between me and them. I told Callum about my attraction to you. Before I called you, I told him that I felt like I missed an opportunity to talk to you about it when I walked you to your door and then left before saying anything."

"What did he say?"

"He pretty much told me that I was a fool. He has never seen me lose confidence before in our lives. To him, that meant that there was something special about you. I already knew that because I've been fighting it, as I told you. He doesn't know that I'm here. I think he knew that I would be. Even more than Tellum, Callum knows me the best. He knows how women are a weakness for me. When it comes to you, you are the greatest of my weaknesses. I have women all around me. It's you that I want. Now, I don't and can't make a promise of forever. I'm sorry if that sounds crass."

"I know all about that where you're concerned. I have ordered many floral arrangements and beautiful pieces of jewelry for women for you, after. I'm not new or green here. I also know what women say about you. Before you ask, it's all good. I've never heard anything bad about your treatment of women. More than anything, those you've been with proclaim that they've never experienced an...well, a..."

He finished for her. He loved her innocence.

"An orgasm? An explosive release? Sexual relief? Shall I give a few more words of what I think you're trying to say? I've heard them. They are flattering. I always, always aim to please. I am not shy about how much I love being with a woman; inside of one. Two consenting adults can have the orgasms of their lives; greater than their imaginations. There is nothing wrong with that," he explained.

Keiko's eyes focused on the floor. Something was wrong. He walked up to her and raised her head with his index finger.

"Talk to me. We said all on the table," he encouraged. "I want you. Have no doubt about that."

Byrum looked down to where his hardness formed a tent in his sweat pants. He wasn't sure she saw it, so he encouraged her to look down. Her eyes widened again before she looked back up at him.

"I don't doubt it. I feel good about it knowing that what I thought I've been seeing and feeling from you is what I hoped it was."

"What's the concern, if there is any?"

"I'm not like the women you are used to. I'm not as... experienced as they are at pleasing a man. I know that sounds odd since I've been married before. That time in my life was not a great experience; at least not for me. What I got out of it was a son. I never reached...well, I've never had... an... orgasm that I didn't give to myself."

Byrum stood stoic. He wasn't sure he was hearing her correctly.

"Keiko, how could a man be married to you and not make sure you were fulfilled first? I don't question you; I question who the hell is he? I know who he is, DeConnor. I just can't see any man taking pleasure and leaving a woman unsatisfied. I know your marriage was rough. I hope that one day, you will trust me enough to talk to me about it if you want to. Outside of boss and employee, I consider you a friend. I've said that plenty of times before."

"You have. We are friends. That's the only way I could be standing here with you. I do want you."

Moving even closer to her until his body was pressed against hers, Byrum put his hands on the door on either side of her and leaned into her lips. He didn't kiss her. He simply wanted her to feel his closeness and hear him when he spoke.

"Keiko, whatever your experience has been in the past, I want you to wipe that from your head. This rendezvous between us tonight will be about you. I know how to derive pleasure for myself. My golden rule with a woman is that she will never, ever, ever leave a bed that she's been in with me and not be completely, totally, wholly, entirely satisfied. Now that I know that sex hasn't been the greatest for you, I have a job to do. I will take your pleasure seriously. If this is the only time that you and I will have together like this, I want to be sure that you know longer have to dream about it or imagine it. You will be able to recall it over and over."

"Whew," Keiko said.

He saw her hands lower where she placed them flat against the door. He smiled against her cheek.

"Touch me anywhere you want. You have the power. You never have to brace yourself on a hard door, unless..."

Byrum didn't finish. The image was enough for him.

"Unless...what?" Keiko asked.

He heard her voice cracking. There was lump in her throat that spoke to her desire to hear much more. He leaned in closer to her hear.

"Unless I'm behind you with your hands planted on a door or wall with me entering you from behind. Bold is who I am, sweetheart."

He licked her earlobe for added measure and pleasure. Keiko's breath hitched. He heard every delicious sound that came from her.

"I can touch you anywhere?" she whispered against his face.

"You are free to touch any and every part of me if that's what you want. Can I kiss you?"

With barely a breath after his question, Keiko blurted out her reply.

"Yes! I wish you would so that I don't die on this hill of need and fall to the floor like a lump of clay," she moaned out, leaving no doubt that she was aroused.

Byrum smiled when he felt her hand on his chest. When she moved it around in circles, he planted a soft kiss on the side of her face.

"Was that, okay?"

He was purposely treading lightly.

"Yyyeesss," she slightly uttered.

Moving his head back, he moved to the left and kissed her sweetly on the lips.

"That?" he said against them.

"More?" Keiko asked.

"Absolutely. All of your wishes are my desires for you tonight."

No more words, Byrum thought as he tasted her lips, giving her a taste and feel of his. His plan was to make sure there wasn't a part of her body that his lips wouldn't touch before the night was over. If he was going to have this one night with her, they would each get their fill.

Byrum moaned against her lips and then into her soft, pliant mouth when she parted her lips ever so slightly. He didn't have to coax her to give him access to more of her lips and the sweetness that lies beyond them. She kissed him back passionately, without any hesitation. The way they were going at each other's lips, the delicious need for each other was evident.

Sliding his tongue between her lips, he swooned when her approval came in the form of her aggressively kissing him back, getting from his mouth and tongue what she needed.

Keiko tasted all kinds of sweet and the thrill of it had him reaching down to pick her up. They had spent enough time at the door.

Her arms gathered around his neck in tandem with her legs which slid around his hips.

The kiss consumed all of him. Months and months of wondering what her lips felt and tasted like had finally become an answered question. She tasted like pure joy; heavenly. One firm thrust after another of their tongues mingling and getting to know each other sent his mind and body reeling with a ferocious need. He had to find a bed.

"Bed?" he asked.

"Now!" Keiko yelled.

Byrum chuckled and made his way across the room. The night was young. His need was animalistic. His desire was for her; and only her.

4

Was this real? Is this happening? Was she really being held in Byrum's arms and on her way to a soft bed which held the promise of passion she's never experienced before?

Keiko had so many thoughts flowing through her mind as Byrum walked the few steps to her bed. She didn't know whether it took seconds, minutes or hours because she was too busy kissing him like a ravenous woman. His lips felt so good against hers. She'd never been this thoroughly kissed before. With her legs around him tight, she felt Byrum's hands sweep up and down her back until his hands went under her nightie where he cupped her behind and squeezed. The delightful intimate gesture caused her hips to flex up, down and around in little circles all on their own. Her mind and her need for him led the way to her response to him. That part of him that she'd heard women glowingly rave about rested hard between them.

"All of you feels like a lot of you," she moaned against his cheek.

Byrum released her lips and moved them down to her neck to kiss along the soft skin he found there.

"It is. I promise you that we will fit together perfectly."

He kissed her again, unraveling any doubt that she was making a mistake allowing him inside of her room and hopefully soon, inside of her body. His kisses spoke of addictive delight for hours to come. She couldn't wait to experience all of him.

When he placed her on the floor and reached for his shirt, she stopped him with her hands. In her past, she'd never been allowed to take any kind of lead. She knew with Byrum that his goal was on her needs and not just his own. She looked into his eyes and the signs of heated passion she saw fueled her desire to just be a part of the moment. She wanted to be a vibrant participant.

"I want to undress you," she said. "I want to see."

"Lights on?" he asked.

"Yes."

Byrum flipped the switch on the wall and the room lit up like the middle of the day. She didn't care. Getting her eyes on what he's been keeping under those suits was important in this moment. She wasn't ready to tell him why.

"Keiko, tell me something," he said to her.

"What?"

Even though he wanted to talk, that didn't stop her from rubbing her hands up and down his strong, muscly arms. She pulled his t-shirt from inside of his sweat pants and slid her hands up and over his bare chest. He felt hard and soft at the same time. The fire within her burned hotter.

"I don't care what your sex life was like with your ex-husband. With me, you get to explore. I already told you that you can touch, kiss, lick – whatever you want. It's just you and me in this room."

"I get that. It's just that I can't begin to tell you how long I've wanted to be here with you like this."

"That feeling is mutual. I'm going to try and not behave like a high school boy our first time, but no promises. You're so damn sexy that I want to get right to the good part."

"So do I. Whew! You have no idea at all," she smiled.

Pulling on his shirt, she pushed it up his body, with his help, until he pulled it over his head and tossed it to the floor. He had a thin gold link chain around his neck. She'd seen it many times before, but never against his bare chest. It looked better than ever before.

When she linked her fingers with his, she could feel the same style chain on his wrist. After rubbing her fingers across it a few times, she let go of any nervousness about what to and not to do. She decided to go for what her mind and body told her she wanted. She pressed her cheek against his bare chest before turning her head to place kisses across it. She closed her eyes and took in the feel of him against her tongue. When he groaned out his approval, she felt powerful. The force of their attraction to one another rocked her to her core. How did she survive wanting him this much and not having him? She no longer needed to torture herself with longing. He was giving himself to her. She accepted the challenge of making this a night to remember; not just for her but for him as well.

Their eyes locked and a burning need gripped her heart and held on tight. This was about to be more than just sex. She kept that thought quietly to herself for now.

With her hands, she reached to the edge of his sweat pants to pull them down. Before she did, she waited while he reached into his pocket, took out the contents and placed everything on the night stand. Her eyes captured a black and gold box and knew what they were.

"I'm always safe. I didn't want to get here and need them and not have them," Byrum explained.

He must have seen the look on her face when she saw the condoms.

"I'm glad you thought of them. I would be some kind of mad to be standing here with you like this only to find we would have to stop."

"No stopping on my end. I've wanted you for too long," he admitted.

Leaning up on her toes as far as she could, she kissed him when he came the rest of the way to meet her. His hands went to her head, gripping her hair, holding her to him. She gripped his pants and moved them down over his slim hips. Pulling on the front, she had to stretch them in order to slide them down beyond his penis where it strained at attention in her direction. Leaving the pants where they were, she couldn't resist touching him there with both of her small hands. She needed both in order to get her hands wrapped all the way around his rigid, steely flesh. She cupped as much of him as she could. She wanted to get acquainted with how thick and heavy he felt under her touch. She looked up when he sighed and dropped his head back the moment she stroked him. The mushroom head of his erection was soft, hard and slippery to her touch.

"You are everything I knew you would be," she blurted out with a craving that had her own body slippery in the right spot.

"Baby, tonight, I am all yours," Byrum gasped out.

She felt his hips moving slightly, aiding her in her strokes. Feeling him slide between her hands made her impatient for him to slide this way in another part of her body.

She had to stop to let him slide his sneakers off and then his sweat pants and boxers. The man of her dreams stood before her completely naked and unashamed about it. She loved a confident man. Seeing all of him, he had a right to be confident and cocky. When she thought of that last word, her first thought was, he had a lot of that.

On one last noisy exhale of pleasure, Byrum removed her hands and picked her up.

"I wasn't doing it right?" she questioned.

"Hell, you were too good at it. I love your hands on me. Trust me, there will be so much more time tonight for you to put your hands on me again. The issue is, I'm completely naked and you have on too many clothes. I want to remedy that. As much as I love all of this red satiny stuff, I've had a look, love what I see but I want you as naked as I am. You good with that? And let me just say that you touching me like that is never a bad thing. Watching these perfectly manicured nails on me and feeling how you perfectly stroke me was too good. I've never prematurely released before. I was close to doing that. The fact that it's you touching me was a salaciously erotic scene. More to come, sweetness."

Keiko felt her body being placed on the bed with Byrum joining her. With her lying flat, he kissed her lips before moving to her shoulder as he slid her robe from her body, kissing it down her arms. She could feel her nipples pebbling under the silky gown. Byrum reached down and pulled it up and over her head, leaving her in a skimpy pair of panties. It suddenly occurred to her that she was about to be naked, in a bed with Byrum Blackstone. Her body was just as aroused as her thoughts were.

Her breath hitched when Byrum methodically stroked a finger across the material between her legs.

"You're soaking wet, Keiko. Later, we'll talk about the thoughts you had getting to this. You're all slippery and wet," he crooned against her neck, straddling her body as he moved his finger up, down and between her moist folds.

She'd never felt so waywardly sexy before. His finger worked like sexy magic on her. If she could stop her hips from moving in sync with his strokes, she wouldn't. Her body quivered all over.

When he covered her mouth in a deep, sensational, penetrating kiss, she gripped his forearms and held on. Byrum leaned down and rained kisses across her chest, allowing one nipple and then the other to slide around in his mouth. When he gripped one with his fingers and the other with his teeth, Keiko felt her body jerk as her body shuddered in a sexy way with the moves of a porn star. She hadn't seen a lot of those movies, but she'd seen enough to know this is what happens when a woman gives into the moment and allows her body to enjoy the spicy attention and affection.

With one finger still stroking inside of her body, with a sexual haze over her vision, she saw Byrum reach for a condom, making haste with getting it on.

He put his full body over hers, kissing her with a hunger that teased and coaxed her to open her legs wide in preparation for what was next.

Reaching down, he quickly and frantically pulled her panties down and off. In a desperate frenzy, Byrum locked onto her tongue, sucking it into his mouth before she joined in the love making their mouths were doing. She sucked on his tongue and discovered the delight it gave her. She was focused on that when with quick, yet firm thrusts, he slid inside of her body. She loved how he gave her a little bit of him at a time, allowing her the chance to get used to his large size fitting inside of her small body. Byrum deliciously fit inside of her, expertly making sure that she could feel every single delectable inch of him.

"Byrum," she moaned, tossing her head from side to side, her long hair flailing about around her. Electricity in waves were flowing from him to her.

Before she could reach to grip his shoulders for a better grip on her lower body, he gathered both of her hands in his and raised them above her head. Feeling out of control with need, she feasted on his mouth. The sounds of them pleasurably moaning and groaning stimulating her even more. The sexy moans signaled how they fabulously mated with a powerful need for each other.

"Keiko, Keiko, Keiko," Byrum repeated over and over.

"I'm here, baby," she replied sexily when his head moved to her chest. His tongue made great work of covering as much skin as his mouth could reach.

With the pure sweet, intoxicating friction their bodies derived, Byrum moved deeper and yet, ever more so deeper into her body. Her hips met him stroke for stroke. When he reached down and moved one of her legs over his shoulder before he leaned up higher for what she now felt was an even deeper stroke, she couldn't hold in her screams of pleasure. She didn't know what the hell was happening to her. Her body felt like it was floating. There was a sudden surge through her that was familiar but only at times when she pleasured herself. She knew what she was feeling but what was coming was stronger and much more powerful.

Byrum's grunts and strokes teased every ember in her body. A murmuring sound escaped her lips, shattering the quiet of the room beyond the fiery sounds of their lovemaking. She embraced herself for the titillating sensation that was setting her body ablaze. As Byrum pumped away inside of her, the bed squeaked. Every part of his body that she touched was slippery with his sweat. She tried to hold back the uninhibited orgasm that was teetering on breaking her into a billion little pieces.

Her breasts tightened. Her hips pumped wildly, matching Byrum as he grunted and surged seductively with a sexually laced grind until she couldn't hold on anymore. The hottest, sexiest guy she's ever seen was loving her. That alone had her welcoming her climax that dizzily blinded her with sparks that went off all around her head and through her body. Embers fired again and again. Her screams couldn't be masked or contained. Keiko heard herself murmuring out her pleasure. Byrum leaned his head back and howled without stopping his loving her in true stallion style. He indeed rode her straight into a state of orgasmic bliss when her released hammered at her body.

It went on and on when Byrum leaned down and nipped at her neck with his teeth. The sensual feelings flowed from those points to her womanhood, sending her spiraling again and again. She couldn't control her hips or her yelps. Heatwave after heatwave crashed into her. She held onto Byrum as his own release hit him again and again when his powerful strokes moved her up the bed. Still, he didn't stop giving them the joy they both sought the minute they revealed how much they wanted and needed each other.

As her body began to float back down to earth and solidly on the bed, she tried to soothe Byrum by rubbing his back and his head. Once he collapsed, slipping his head between her head and her shoulder, she held him close. She could feel him trying to hold off on putting his full weight on her. Once he released her leg, she used them to pull him down on her fully. She loved the feel of him covering her from head to toe.

Turning them over so that they were facing each other, she brushed a sweet kiss against the hollow area of his neck. In her attempt to wipe the sweat from his brow as they tried to control their breathing, he took her hand and kissed each finger before placing her hand over his heart.

The air around them was filled with the scent of their love. She inhaled sharply to get more of it.

"Keiko, I wasn't expecting that to happen. By that, I mean, my body had its own mine beyond my control. I felt like a wild animal who couldn't seem to get enough of its mate. Was I too hard? Too rough?"

Keiko kissed his lips. She kept hers on his for more than a minute.

"You were hard when and where you needed to be as well as where I wanted you to be. Byrum, you did something for me tonight."

"What?" he asked, his hand rubbing across her hip and around to her behind.

"You proved to me that I can have an orgasm during sex and not just during masturbation. I have so much I'd like to share but I won't right now. I want to bask in this afterglow. How many condoms did you bring?" she asked.

Keiko faked looking over his shoulder at the nightstand.

"Four and we're going to use them all before you kick me out of your bed. I've got plans for you; for us. We have more orgasms to get to."

Keiko laughed out loud. She shivered as her released continued to grab hold of her. She never wanted to let it go.

"Music to all parts of my body!" she cheered.

**

Keiko woke with the sun beaming in her eyes. She was turned

on her side with Byrum close behind her. She remembered why the blinds and curtain were open instead of closed like they were when she first arrived back to her room after leaving the wedding reception. When her mind took her there, she trembled. Her body was in tune with her mind when it came to the events of the night before.

After the countless number of unforgettable, mind-blowing, body shattering orgasms she'd had, she had come out of the bathroom to find Byrum standing naked, looking out over the Detroit night sky. She walked up behind him, wrapping her arms around his body. Feeling a level of comfort she'd never had with a man before, she spread opened mouth kisses across his back. When he moved her hands down his body to that part of him that had given her pleasure beyond her belief, she kept her hands there and moved them over him, up and down in a slow motion that fused fire intoxicatingly from him to her. From the feel of him, without words, she knew that there was more to come. He promised her a full night of pleasure. He was up and ready in every way.

Byrum then pulled a pillow from the bed and placed it on the ledge of the window. He picked her up and sat her on it, making sure she didn't feel the hard surface under it. She thought that he would open her legs and enter her as he had done twice so far. Instead, he kissed her savagely, the way that he now knew she loved. She didn't know it herself until he introduced her to that kind of delectable mouth-mating. He then slid down to the floor, lifted her legs up and onto his shoulders. After winking at her with a sexy smirk on his face, she knew his intentions. This would be the third time tonight that he'd pleasured her with his mouth; something she'd never had done to her before Byrum. That was a topic that he promised they would have to talk about at another time. With her back planted against the window with the blinds opened, Byrum showed her what none of her dreams about him could have prepared her for. His head went between her legs and she experienced pure ecstasy.

In the light of day, she thought about all that they had done together and didn't know who she was. The sex had been wild. It had been better than great. There was no doubt that it would be. It was now a new day. The night was over. What he'd promised her was fulfilled. Fear was setting in. The things they'd done made it hard for her to think about facing him. What kind of insatiable she-devil did she give birth to the night before? She was a woman she didn't know existed. She loved every minute of that part of her that Byrum pulled out of her. Her need for him was unquenchable. Her body craved him again and again. What now? How could she look at him after their night? She was embarrassed. She had to escape before he woke up.

Trying hard to not wake him, Keiko slid her body forward until she was on the edge of the bed. Byrum's arm fell from her body and onto the bed. The moment her feet touched the floor, an ache between her legs was an even bigger reminder of the workout they gave the bed and her body. It wasn't a pain that she didn't want. In fact, she loved it.

Standing she looked around for her clothes and couldn't seem to find them. How was she going to escape if she couldn't get to her clothes?

"Sweetheart, this is your room. You can't run away. I know that's what you're doing."

Keiko stopped in her tracks. Her plan to not wake Byrum did not pan out that way.

She turned in his direction. Still stark naked, she saw her red robe at the foot of the bed and grabbed it.

"Um, hey. Or, good morning. Should I say hello?" she stammered out.

Byrum rolled over on his back, placing his hands under his head and laughed.

"You are so beautiful. Please tell me you are not going back to being shy around me? Last night?"

Keiko raised her hand to stop him from saying more.

"I know I sound ridiculous. I must look crazy trying to run from my own room. You caught me. I was remembering last night and, wow."

"Wow good? Wow, not so good? Wow, you want to do it again?" he asked.

She relaxed and laughed. That was his intention and he achieved it. She calmed.

"I confess. I had the best time of my entire life with you last night; the whole night. I think the sun was coming up after that last time on the window ledge. I'm glad you carried me to the bed because walking was not going to be possible."

"You being satisfied is all I need to know. I don't want you to be ashamed or shy about last night. We got what we came together for."

Keiko nodded and slid her robe on, tying it around her waist.

"We did. Thank you for last night. I never knew sex could be that good, and adventurous, and wild, and amazing, and earth-shattering, and wonderful. I didn't know my body could do such things."

"Oh, no. What have we unleashed in you?" Byrum kidded.

"I don't know but I liked that, Keiko."

"I like every Keiko."

"Byrum, what now?"

He moved the comforter from over his body showing her that even though it was a new day, the night wasn't over yet. He was ready for more.

"Are you in a rush?" he asked.

Reaching to the night-stand, he showed her the last of the four condoms that he'd brought with him.

No way was she going to pass up the chance for a little more of Byrum Blackstone. If she had to take this night with her to the grave one day, she was going to drain it dry.

Removing her robe, she slid back into bed and rolled over on top of him. Taking the condom from his hand, she ripped it open with her teeth.

"I'll hold onto this. Show me," she said.

"Show you?"

"Show me how to please you by..."

Keiko wasn't ready to say the words yet. The one thing they hadn't done throughout the night and he didn't press her to do it, was for her to taste that part of him that had spent most of the night inside of her. She would sheath him when the time came for more. He'd turned her out in every way possible but that one. She wanted it. She wanted him.

Moving the comforter from the bed all together, Keiko slid down his body while her eyes stayed locked on his. Channeling the lascivious woman from the night before, she did what he told her she could always do with him. She went for what she wanted.

5

"Everybody, settle down; settled down please."

Byrum waved his hand across the crowd in the conference room to quiet all of the individual conversations. He removed his suit jacket and placed it over the back of his chair at the end of long black and silver, glass-topped, rectangle conference room table. Rather than continue to stand behind the chair, he sat in hopes that everyone would calm down if they saw that he was calm and ready to continue with their team meeting. There had been several issues on the island during his absence while he attended Tellum and Cheyenne's wedding in Detroit. Now that he was back, several teams wanted to bring him up to speed on what the latest around their work was and how they were moving forward through any issues that may have come up.

Byrum looked around the table at his leadership team and wondered why they hadn't dealt with these issues themselves. He'd been back a little over a week and already he was being hit from the left and right with things he hoped someone else could deal with.

With Tellum still on his honeymoon and Callum off to Hawaii to check on the development of *Quiet Whisper*, their third of the three resorts, he and the leaders around the table were left to make all of the decisions.

"Byrum, I think I've taken care of the food delivery that

looked like it was going to be an issue."

Byrum leaned back in his chair, crossed his legs at the knee and was hoping he could scratch one item off of his list when it came to placing an extra push on the vendor.

"Let's hear it," he said to Jeff, one of the guys who had been on the island from the beginning of the construction which began over a year ago. Jeff was a native of the island and knew his way around after working at one of the other larger resorts. That one was a family resort. Like *Secret Whisper, Silent Whisper* would be an adult only resort.

"The license for the alcohol was a problem. There was paperwork that was due over a week ago, a day after you left the island. I will take the blame for it not getting completed and turned in on time. Elsa did everything she was supposed to do."

"Do we have an issue right now with the license? You know how much alcohol we'll need on a daily basis. There can't be any slipups or oversights. That's why I hired you. If that's going to be a problem going forward, let me know now."

The stern warning Byrum had just issued was not his usual demeanor. At this point, he had to be more pointed in his approach to be sure everyone was doing their best. They were paid handsomely to do so. His expectations were high.

"I got it. Just before this meeting, I checked and we're all good. It's no longer an issue. I didn't have time to reach out to Keiko to have it removed from the meeting's agenda. I know she's just getting back today. I didn't want to overwhelm her."

Hearing her name, Byrum shifted in his chair. He looked to his right at the far end of the table and there she was looking like pure perfection. Even though she was an impeccably dressed as she always was, he couldn't stop seeing images of

Keiko naked and writhing around underneath of him like an uninhibited sex kitten; his sex kitten.

They had barely gotten any sleep that night they spent together. Since then, they hadn't been in contact. He wanted to give her space as they figured out how to navigate this new connection now that they'd had sex. He had to wonder, was it really just sex? Maybe it was more?

After leaving her hotel room that afternoon, all he'd been able to think about was how to convince Keiko that their one-night-stand would be torture if he didn't get a second night; perhaps even a third and fourth. Hell, he would take *anything* she was willing to do with him as long as the answer wasn't nothing at all. His desire for her couldn't handle zero intimacy.

His lips turned up into a slight smile at the way Keiko tried to avoid looking at him. He would address that later. There was no doubt in his mind that she was having the same thoughts that he was.

"Make sure you provide Keiko with a final copy of the contract. What about the event planner? I would love to scoop up the one who does all of the events at *Secret Whisper* but Tellum would have a cow. I like poking that bear, so let's try that route. I saw on the agenda that the vendor wanted to make some adjustments to the contract that were not agreed upon. Marcia?"

Byrum and everyone else in the room turned to a member of his marketing and promotions team who had taken on the task of leading the team to secure the event planner. If they could get the planner for their grand opening who worked at *Secret Whisper*, he was fine with a new vendor for ongoing events.

"Right. My turn. Well, we were good to go, as you know, before you left to attend the wedding. I was expecting the signed contract back from her attorney a few days after that. Two days ago, I received an updated contract with changes that I think are outrageous. I wasn't sure if you wanted to take this to the senior leadership team to decide whether to accept or deny any of her additional requests."

"I want you to decide what to do. If what she's asking for seems a little off-kilter, decline the updates and go to the next vendor on the list. There were five contenders. Each of the other four would be happy to have the contract we offered her."

Byrum looked at his iPad for the next item that should have been handled without his input.

"Guys, listen, I'm looking at these lists of issues and I expect my leaders to do better than to come to me with the menial things. I trust your judgement. I want you to go back to your team meetings and fix whatever you think needs my eyes but doesn't really. I have a lot to get to in the few days I'll be here before I need to fly out to Denver to a meeting. I was hoping to return and be brought up to date without me making decisions that aren't about major money or big reconstruction issues. I did do a walkthrough early this morning while I did my morning run. I love that the pools are all done. I had one of the men turn the pool lights on for me. They'll be great at night. I'd like to see the report on the over-the-water bungalows. This resort was originally created from a reconstructed 19th-century fortress. I love that we've kept some of those touches. One of the big draws for this resort are the wide subterranean winding paths. There are also the romantic suites that are positioned on a cliff overlooking the ocean. My flight back to the island took me that way. I must say, it's a flawless view. I'd like my weekly report to include how close we are to those suites being completed. I'd like to take a close look at those. From what I've been told, they are still roped off on the base level at the elevators. That's fine, but we should be ahead on those. You all have made remarkable progress. I think I have the best teams of my brothers and their teams. Let's keep it that way. Let's blow the other resorts out of the park when it comes to the sensationalism. The bigger the bang, the bigger the bonuses. Keep that in mind. Unless there is anything else urgent, I'll keep an eye out for updates for tomorrow's report. If you need to see me directly, please schedule some time through Keiko or Sarai before I leave. Sarai is Keiko's assistant, so don't drop everything on her. Run by Keiko what you would normally let her get first. She'll assign to Sarai what she'd like her to handle. Are we clear?"

Byrum looked at the thumbs up and head nods around the table.

"Anything else?" Keiko asked everyone. "I know I'm just back in the office today. I did look over a lot of your reports last night after I got in. Before you schedule meetings with Byrum, please schedule fifteen minutes with me first. Byrum, if you have a few minutes, I'd like to speak with you to go over your travel schedule. Callum has the private jet. I want to be sure the accommodations I have for your flight to Denver work for you."

Byrum didn't answer immediately. He loved that he was able to set his eyes on her without feeling the need to look away if anyone caught him looking at her a little too long.

"Byrum?"

He heard Jeff's voice and coughed to focus his brain off of the way Keiko's mouth let's out tiny shrieks when she orgasms. He shook it off.

"Oh, yes, that's fine. I'll meet you in my office when we're done. I'm hoping that's now?"

"I do have one more thing," Keiko said.

Byrum nodded at her.

"The floor is yours," he said.

"I know we asked for five volunteers to spend the night in the new cabanas on the beach. We also have one bungalow ready for someone to stay in and give us feedback. I did the lottery for those slots last night. Thanks to everyone who submitted a request. We really need your feedback as the construction continues. Make sure your observations are from the mind of a visitor and not a worker. Check your email. I've set up a meeting tomorrow in the afternoon with everyone who'll be staying in them. The only part that won't be available are the fire pits. Those have to be monitored closely. We're reserving that until we're close to opening. Any questions?" Keiko asked.

Byrum's mind went to how he would like to spend a night in one of the cabanas with Keiko, or in one the bungalows. He wanted to sink inside of her under the stars. He wanted the chance. Would he ever get to that day? He didn't know. The way they left things, they were done. To him, those were only words. He had every intention of proposing a counter offer to their one night. He hoped he could get to it before he flew to Denver to meet up with Callum for a business forum.

"Okay, everyone – thanks for the hard work. I'll be in my office for the rest of the day and probably most of the evening. If you need me, that's where you'll find me. Tomorrow is a full day and I don't have much availability. Check with Keiko."

Everyone stood to leave except for him. As they exited the room, he kept his eye on Keiko. He wanted her to look back at him as she left the room. He wanted, needed a sign that they weren't going to go back to business as usual. Business he could handle. It was the pleasure that he needed more of. He hoped beyond all hope that she did too. They'd made love four times in one night. That was definitely a record for him. That didn't even include the times he spent with his head between her legs or hers between his. The idea of it had his body hardening in places that he didn't want to be obvious to his staff. How could they have a marathon like that with a craving for more and then walk away? He couldn't. Maybe Keiko couldn't either.

He stood, put his suit jacket back on and grabbed his items from the table. He was about to find out.

6

Keiko looked up from where her eyes were looking over the work schedule for the staff for the next two weeks. Her main focus was on those who would be off the island. She needed to be sure that all shifts were covered before final requests for leave away from the office were approved. Her eyes caught sight of Byrum as he headed toward his office after greeting everyone he hadn't had a chance to converse with since he returned to the island.

Unlike her, he had returned several days ago. She spent her time after their rendezvous in the hotel with Tru and her parents. The fact that DeConnor was around for some of that didn't bother her the way that it had in the past since their divorce. His presence used to annoy her; pretty much intimidate her as he'd done throughout their marriage. She felt free now. Being with Byrum also helped her feel that way. His biggest impact was in the bedroom; big being the prominent word because he was that and then some. She still had a feeling between her legs that reminded her how passionate he'd loved on her and her on him. Her every waking hour was on how fantastic sex could be with the right person.

Her sexual desires had been stifled for years. She hadn't had a lot of experience before DeConnor, unlike some of her friends who had wild stories of their sexual exploits to share with her. She wanted to have that kind of fun when it came to sex. DeConnor wouldn't hear of it. He had an image of sex with his wife that was tamer than what she now knew was his way of controlling her. After Byrum, she was going through withdrawal. The desire to make herself orgasm with his face in mind almost had her caving in to do so. That's not what she wanted. She wanted him, but she couldn't have him. That wasn't possible now that they were back on the island. What they shared was for that one night only. She'd been going stir-crazy for those feelings since then.

When she arrived in the conference room for the morning meeting, it was agony not being able to hug, kiss and hold him. Kissing. She wanted the kissing. Each time he spoke, she couldn't help herself from looking at his lips and remembering all the ways they had pleased her.

"You coming?" Byrum said as he walked up.

Keiko shook off her nostalgic moment when Byrum showed up at her office door. He did not have to say those words.

"What?" she asked when the image of herself and him doing just that clouded her mind.

"You wanted to talk to me? You looked like you were a million miles away. You ready?"

Keiko fumbled around with papers on her desk. She didn't care why. She needed a moment to gather herself.

"Oh, yes. I'm on my way."

Byrum walked off to his office. She grabbed a few things from her desk and headed in his direction. Before doing so, she straightened her dress and pulled her hair back out of her face. As she walked by the mirror on the wall next to her office door, she stopped and checked her hair and makeup.

"Stop it, Keiko," she mumbled to herself.

She hated that she was acting nothing like she usually would.

"Ugh," she grumbled and then left her office.

When she arrived at Byrum's office, she knocked on the opened door. She moved inside when he looked up and found her standing there. Any other time, she would walk in and go right up to this desk to discuss whatever was on her mind. Everything about their interaction was different now.

She walked inside on unstable legs even though she didn't have on her usual five-inch heels. The moment she arrived at his desk, she looked back over her shoulder at all the traffic outside of the office. She backed up and closed the office door. She then closed the blind on the one, small window in his office that allowed him to see the open office space on the other side of the door. When she heard him chuckle, she turned in his direction.

"Keiko, are you a spy? Do you know of a spy? What are you doing?" he asked jokingly.

"It's not funny, Byrum. Are people talking or whispering about us? You've been back a few days. What have you heard?" she whispered.

When Byrum tried to respond by whispering back at her, she moved closer to him to hear what he had to say.

"Can you hear me?" he uttered softly. "I'm talking low because it's pretty crazy that you are whispering. I don't know if you plan to talk about state secrets or what," he kidded even more.

Keiko felt her heart drop. Was he being serious? She got her answer when he leaned back and laughed harder.

"Stop laughing, Byrum. This is serious."

"No, it's not. You're being over the top. You don't have to do that. No one is talking about you or me or you and me. Keiko, you're acting like you stole the Hope diamond or something. Do you have it hidden underneath of that dress? Can I check?"

She heard her name and snapped out of it. Not knowing what else to do, she finally laughed at herself. She must look ridiculous; and suspicious.

"Stop me from embarrassing myself. I know I'm acting weird. It's just that we had, you know."

"Can we stop whispering? I am quite sure no one is at the door trying to listen through the slit at the bottom of it. I can't wait until our permanent office space is ready in a few weeks. I can't believe the old owner had people working in this building on the regular. My new office will have a whole lot of privacy. Now, can I start by saying hello and asking how you're doing? We haven't talked since I left your hotel room. You know, after we had...um...sex," he said, mocking her attempt to say the word but didn't.

She started to look back at the door again the minute he said the word, sex. That would only lead her to act out of character once again. She fought the temptation to look. She relaxed her shoulders. Sitting down would help, but her legs wouldn't stop pacing.

"I'm not okay. I'm a ball of nervousness," she finally said.

"Why?"

She placed her hand on her hips while trying to understand why she's the only one of the two of them who seemed to care about being found out.

"Why? Didn't you hear me? We had sex, Byrum."

"No, I said sex. You didn't say it at all. It's not a dirty word.

In fact, it's damn near erotic when I think of all that you did to me in that hotel room."

"Stop it. We can't keep remembering that, especially in the office," she exclaimed.

"Mmmm, of course I remember that. It's all I can think about. Well, that and what kind and color of panties you have on under that dress."

Keiko widened her eyes at his attempt to get a rise out of her. She didn't understand why he was taking things so lightly.

"I'm a mess, Byrum. Stop laughing and cracking jokes."

"I asked how you were doing. You said you're not okay. I want to know why. You didn't have a good time with me?"

"I had a great time. The best time of my life. I mean, four times to start with. I could barely move around for the rest of that day. That wasn't a bad thing at all. There was nothing bad about that night or that morning."

"So, you felt me all day long?"

"I swear, I think I still do. I know this sounds crazy to ask but, is that normal for you because how the hell does a woman keep up with you, if so?"

"It was you. I couldn't stop desiring you knowing that we had agreed to that one night. I guess I was thinking that was it. Was it?"

Keiko had been wondering the same thing. She had been craving his touch and his kiss.

"We said it was. We can't do that here. It's too risky."

"You really want to stop? The way you rocked my world – you can't decide that nothing else can happen between us."

"We said one night in order to get each other out of our systems."

"Keiko, you are not out of my system. In fact, the more

days that go by the more stir-crazy I am."

"I spent three days being unable to focus, especially at night. I stayed with Madison my last night and I tossed and turned in her guest bedroom. I wanted to feel you reach for me," she finally admitted.

"See? Was that so hard? I can admit that I missed you. I was excited knowing that you would be back today. I don't want you to worry about people knowing. How could they? We were in Detroit. No one saw me leaving your room. It was between us. Just as it would be if you found some time for me when I return from Denver. I'll only be there one day."

"Byrum, as much as I really want to, and I mean I really do, I don't think we should. This resort is a small community."

"And what would they talk about? You and me in my office with the door closed? We do that all the time. There is nothing else for them to know unless you or I say something. I'm never going to say anything. I also believe that we don't have to stop indulging. When I don't stay here on the resort in the section that's fully completed, I stay in my apartment that's about twenty miles from here. I miss you. I want to see you outside of work. Can we at least talk about it? Do you really want to go back to not letting me lick you all over?" Byrum leaned forward and spoke right to her face.

His face was a whisper away from hers. If she moved forward slightly, their lips could touch.

She wiped the idea from her head and moved away.

"You're a tease," she uttered.

"I am. Can I tease you in private? I promise that I'll even make you dinner. I would say let's get together before I leave, but that may not work. That's how much I want you again."

"Byrum, all those times weren't enough?" she questioned.

"Okay, let me ask you this. Were they enough for you? You don't miss my touch enough to want it despite the risk? Me? I'm not worried at all. I don't want anyone to find out if it will hurt you. As for me, I don't hide who I am. I don't want to hide my desire for you. I get it though. That doesn't take away from the fact that at night, I'm thinking about what I know is under that dress except for the color of your panties. You always wear the sexy kind?"

That got a huge smile from her. They were flirting and no one else besides them was any more the wiser. She kept her eyes on him to make sure he was serious about her answering that. When his eyes appeared to smolder and turn darker, she knew.

"Royal blue."

"Bra and panties?"

"A woman who doesn't match should be shot and flogged! Yes, same color for both. It's a bra and thong though. There is a difference."

"I don't care about there being a difference. I care about whether or not you're going to let me see another colored set. I leave in a day and I return a day later. Have dinner with me at my apartment. I can cook for us. We can decide what to do in that private time. I haven't had enough of you, Keiko. I don't think I ever will. I get your reservations. They are valid. That doesn't make me want you less. In fact, I'm thinking about you sitting on that window ledge with your legs over my shoulders and my head..."

Keiko through her palm up at him to stop him. He was relentless and sexy at it.

"I get it. Ugh, you're killing me with the visual."

"Well, if you could see on the other side of the table, you

would see what that visual is doing to me. I have to get to a meeting in fifteen minutes. If you agree to have dinner with me, I can think of something like the weather and all will be back to normal in my southern region."

Byrum looked down toward his lap and she understood. She also knew that he wasn't the only one of them that was aroused right now. His mouth loved all over her womanly folds. No man had ever done that before. Her ex didn't believe in oral sex on a woman. Byrum seemed to love doing it as much as she enjoyed receiving it.

"What if..."

Byrum stopped her mid-sentence.

"Look, I don't want to make this hard on you. I'm putting this out in the open and on the table for you. Do with it what you want. I want you to know that one night wasn't enough for me. I want more. I can be discreet. I know you can as well. Us being in my office together or in a rideshare together isn't anything new as far as other people would be concerned. Nothing changes in the eyes of those around us. In private, we can do all of the nasty, kinky things we talked about. You told me that you love this newfound, sexual being that you were that night with me. Can you really put her away under lock and key again? I'm offering you more times like that and in the privacy of my place. I want you to think about it. What I don't want is for you to feel pressured. If you aren't interested and I'm out of your system already, I'll have to live with that one night. If that's not the case, I'm going to text you the passcode to get into my apartment. When I return from Denver, I'm going straight home since it will be around eight at night. If you're there, I'll be happy. If not, I'll understand. I won't say it would make me happy to know that you're turning me down. I will say, I get it. You have a couple of days to think about it. We don't have to talk about it anymore. I like you. I didn't think that one night with you would impact me in such a way that I can't stop thinking about you. It has. Just answer me a question. If we were in this building all alone with no one else around, would I be able to have you right here in my office?"

Keiko nodded her answer. She was afraid to speak the words. She was falling for him. They were supposed to have had sex and then moved on from each other. Of course, she wanted him more than just that one night.

"In a heartbeat. My body never felt that good before. And your kisses? It's a lot to think about. We're talking about hooking up here where anyone from work could run into me coming or going to your place."

"Not the first time. They've known you to take a rideshare to my place to bring something urgent that I need to see or something I may have left behind. You're making more out of this because we had sex. Everything is different now. We acted on our carnal desire for one another and now, we want more. You do too, right?"

"I do. You have no idea how much I do."

"Then take a trip on the wild side with me. You won't regret it. I would like to give you a full body sensual massage. I'm no expert but I want to touch your body. You need to relax more, especially when it comes to me. Don't answer me today. If you're there, okay. If you're not, I'll be disappointed but like I said, I get it. There is no pressure to let me take your panties off with my teeth. I digress down from that mountain of pure lasciviousness."

"You're killing me, Byrum. I will think about it. In the

meantime, you have a meeting to get to in less than five minutes. Also, Duron Knight from Pioneer Architecture is trying to reach you about a visit here to discuss the design for the additional two pools with new hotel suites built around it. He mentioned wanting to come out to see the island but his wife is out of town and he has all five of their kids at home. That's where he's working from. He said he can opt into a video chat for now and then perhaps he can get here in about two weeks."

"He and Michael Bailey did mention on my last call with them that they had ideas on the use of the additional land we have that doesn't have anything on it right now. I'm thinking of adding a sports arena where couples can play tennis, pickleball, golf, batting cages and definitely a go-cart track. There is also an idea for a zipline on the opposite side of the mountain with the cliff suites. They're looking ahead to phase two of the construction. Can you set up a call with him in about two hours? I don't know what time it is in Atlanta right now. See what works for him. My flight to Denver all set?"

"I made first class arrangements since the jet isn't here. You mentioned you only needed one way? Are you sure you only want to stay for one night? I know you like to have at least one day to hang out with your friends who live there."

"I want to come back here in hopes that I'll walk into my apartment and you'll be there. If I have a free night, I'm choosing you. I can hang with them another time. As for the jet, yes, I'm meeting Callum there. He's returning to Detroit after the meeting. I'll bring the jet back here with me, so I'm good on the return flight. Soon we won't have this issue anymore. We're adding two more jets. Tellum and my dad are handling that after his honeymoon. They just need to do the final walkthrough with our money guys. He told me to keep this one with me. He and my dad will fly with the other two back to Detroit. Remember the issue we had with the airline? The guy who thought he was going to snatch Cheyenne from Tellum?"

"I do. That was some crazy drama. Anyone who came within a few feet of those two had to know that there was no other woman for Tellum and no other man for Cheyenne."

"Yeah. His father is renting us a private hanger at the airport. We're going to keep the jets there."

"I'm assuming Callum's assistant, Janice, has the information ready for his flight? I'll call her just to be sure. We try to connect once a week, along with Tellum's assistant just to be sure we're on the same page for the three of you when it comes to your travel schedule. Janice also handles the schedule for your father until he hires an assistant."

"And then you'll think about allowing me to show you a good time when I get back?"

When Byrum hit her with that babyface sexy smile, she couldn't resist him. She wouldn't say yes right now, but she would think about it.

"Like you said, if I'm there, remember? I promise I will think about it. I have a lot of work to get to after being on vacation for a week. You need to get out of here and to the other side of the resort for your meeting. I'll see you when you return."

"Naked?" he kidded.

"Cute. Don't tempt me. This new Keiko who throws caution to the wind might continue to accept your challenge."

She turned to leave. When she reached for the door handle, she not only felt but heard his silent gaze as she walked.

"I love a good challenge," he said.

Keiko started to walk out of his office and stopped. She turned back to face him.

"Can I ask you a personal question?"

"You can always and forever ask me anything."

"At one point you wanted to spend most of your time here once the resort was up and running. Detroit would be your second home, this being your homebase. Do you still plan to live here?"

"I don't know anymore. I've been thinking about that. The thing about having money is that you can build a house here and there, pretty much anywhere and it can become home. I'm starting to think that no matter where I am, where I lay my hat, Detroit will have to always be home. My brothers and I talked about that recently. I'm starting to think more about home than house. I'll let you know when I decide."

"That's fair."

"What about you? How long before you decide that it's time for you to get back to Detroit and to Tru?"

"He'll be here with me for the rest of the summer soon. I love it here. There is so much peace away from my old life. I miss my family and my friends. I miss the team at the office back there. I like being with the people here."

"Am I included in that?"

Her answer was immediate.

"Yes. You are why I came here. You are why I stay."

Byrum stood and walked around to her.

"We need to talk when I get back; I mean really talk. I know it was just one night but something was brewing for me when it comes to you way before that night. Even if you don't decide to spend some time with me alone when I return, I want us to talk; heart to heart, not holding anything back. Can I at least get you to agree to that?"

"Yes."

She wanted to say more. There will come a time when she will. Maybe it was time that they talked about more than just desire. Perhaps there could be more. She was already feeling it. It was her secret for now.

Byrum opened the door for her.

"You are beautiful," he leaned over and whispered to her.

Keiko didn't respond. She simply smiled to herself. Definitely more, she thought as she headed back to her office. She prayed she could focus on work and not on the way Byrum looked with his lips all wet and sexy looking when he lifted his head from between her legs.

"It's going to be a long day," she expressed to herself.

7

With *Secret Whisper* coming up on a year that it's up and running, Byrum knew that now was a good time to review the projected profits. He had to review the report more than once to believe that they had turned such a huge profit in such a short amount of time. Each brother had assumed that it would take some time for that to happen. Due to the popularity of their other resorts and the rave reviews that *Secret Whisper* has been getting, the resort has been completely booked week after week.

"You look like you're contemplating the meaning of life over there."

Byrum would normally ignore his brother's attempt at engage him in wild banter. Today was not that day. To him, he was contemplating the meaning of his own life. At least when it came to Keiko.

Since the moment he left the resort without seeing her, she's been on his mind.

"I'm looking over the financials. Are we still doing the additional call with our money guys? We talked about everything with them about the new jets, but I want to dive into these numbers. If they are correct, every resort is in the black, or should I say the green."

"Good, right?" Callum asked. "We are ahead of the game. Tellum knocked it out the park with *Secret Whisper*. You're doing the same, from what I can see, with *Silent Whisper*. His phone rings non-stop with artists looking to perform there. He's thinking of adding more residencies."

"We'll be saying the same about *Quiet Whisper* soon as well. Are we still over a year or so out?"

Callum nodded.

"More like closer to two years. Hawaii is a different circumstance. I want to be sure that we are bringing a lot of jobs, yes, but not disrupting the lives of the people who live there full-time. Pop is flying to Hawaii with me soon to talk with the local politicians and the community group members who want to be sure that we're all on the same page. We're being extremely accommodating. I think that puts us in a good place. I sent you all of their concerns. We can go over them with Tellum. What's on your mind? Since I picked you up on the island, you've been quieter than usual. You've been doing a lot of flying here and there lately. I think you need some down time. You can't keep running like this."

Byrum knew his brother was right.

"There's a lot to do. We haven't had these great successes by sitting still and watching them happen. You, of all people, know what we have to be foot soldiers on the ground and being present. Yes, we can do more meetings virtually but I prefer in-person and so does Tellum. You do also. Don't act like it's just us. With us bringing dad onboard now that he's retired, he's been the lead on all things financial. That's one monkey off of our backs that we don't have to focus on directly. Where is he right now?"

"He's in Los Angeles doing some consulting work. Mom went with him so that they could make a vacation out of it. He's going to show her the house this time?" Callum asked.

Their father decided to surprise their mother with a house in Malibu. They had been scoping one out for a while. Their father knew when their mother had fallen in love with something without her even having to actually say so. They knew each other that well.

"I don't think so. The owner had been using it as an Airbnb. Pop wants to have all of the renovations done before he springs it on her. They're staying at the W in downtown Los Angeles for this trip. One of mom's friends lives there so she'll be occupied until Pop finishes his meetings. What are you up to after Denver? You still heading home to Detroit? I appreciate you coming to pick me up from the resort. Keiko had made plans for me to travel to Denver," Byrum noted.

"I know. I wanted the company. I had some extra time. Kendra is traveling with her team to do some promotional touring. That WNBA schedule has her busy, especially since the season has also begun."

Kendra Grimes was Callum's woman of the moment. She's a professional basketball player who played for the Las Vegas team.

"Y'all been hanging in there pretty tight for a while now. What's going on with that?"

"Nothing. Don't even go there. The only one of us who has no problem being in a committed relationship is Tellum. We see how that ended."

Byrum looked across the plane at Callum who was resting with his feet up on the seat in front of him that faced him. He looked at himself in the same posture.

"Hey, don't knock our brother for falling in love. Cheyenne is our sister now. She's also amazing."

Callum looked in his direction.

"Are you serious, right now? You think that was a complaint? Far from it. I will say, if there is a woman out here like her and she crosses my path, I hope I'm ready to fall head-over-heels like he did. I see you've been quiet about Keiko since the night of the wedding and reception. We've talked a few times and it hasn't come up. What gives? We're on the jet alone. What happened or did you chicken out?"

Byrum was never happier about the fact that he didn't chicken out. If he had, he would not have had the best sex of his life. He was drowning in desire when he should be flourishing in it. The way Callum was looking at him, he wouldn't get away from the conversation without telling it all to him. They still had a few hours before they would land in Denver.

He had been all set with flight arrangements when Callum called and said he was in the air with the jet and on his way to the island. After having the plane checked over and refueled, they got on their way.

"We had a night," was all Byrum said.

He already knew he didn't need to say more for Callum to understand.

"And since then?"

"Nothing."

"Nothing?"

"Bro, you heard me."

"Is that why you've been so grumpy today? You finally got your wish with Keiko and what? You're in love or something now and your heart is broken?"

Byrum let the words live in the air. He hated the 'love' word. The last time he uttered those words, things didn't turn out so well for him. He was left hanging and very much crushed. He looked away from Callum and returned to perusing the reports.

"We should schedule a call with Tellum before we meet about the financials. I want to get his take on plans to expand on *Secret Whisper* in a few years. Duron Knight has reached out about the future plans for the expansion of *Silent Whisper*. I think we should talk about both sites at the same time. I know we're limited on *Quiet Whisper*."

"Yeah, I don't want to touch it. It won't be our largest resort but it will be the most luxurious. I know the cost alone will vet and keep a lot of people from being able to afford it. That's so that we are bringing wealth to the citizens of Hawaii and not just taking up more of their land. It's also our first resort that's not on the water. It's surrounded by mountains on all sides. I know you're trying to distract from my question. I'll give you a few seconds, but then we're back to what I asked you."

"If you say so," Byrum muttered under his breath. He was sure his words were still understood.

"You're in love with her, aren't you? I already know the answer. If you're thinking of not seeking more with Keiko, you're a damn fool. Man, the way you look at her when you think no one is looking is priceless."

"You know my thoughts on that love thing. I'm not doing it again."

"So, you're not in love with her?"

"I am."

Hearing himself say it made him exhale a heavy breath. He'd been holding that in for a long time. Now that he's been with her physically and knows that they are compatible in every way, approaching anything with the idea of it being long-term with her wasn't comfortable ground for him. His mind and body were all over the place. He craved her like a starving man. What he came to realize was that it wasn't only sexual, though that is amazing with her. He wanted all of her, even if it was in small doses. His fear was in scaring her off while also thinking about him getting hurt again. The kind of betrayal that he suffered with Valencia's decision to marry another man still got under his skin in the worse way.

"I know. Does she know?" Callum asked.

"No."

"It's been a week since that night. Why nothing since then? She's back on the island. You were back before she returned."

"There is a lot at risk with her working for me."

"Okay, then fire her and let her work for me. That would fix the problem."

"Hell no!" Byrum yelled as his body stiffened imagining not being around her at all. That would mean Keiko would return to the Detroit office. He selfishly wanted her close.

"Okay, don't take my head off. I was trying to come up with a way to erase that barrier. Why is it an issue anyway? You like each other. I say go for it and screw anyone who has an issue."

"That would be fine if the person with the issue wasn't Keiko. We spent an amazing night together. When I say it defies the description of the word amazing, I mean that. I don't want to scare her with saying I'm in love with her. I don't think she wants that in her life after the horrible marriage she suffered through for years. I wish I could offer her more but I don't know if I really can. I can say I love her but will I really trust myself to not hold a part of me back because of the past?

What about her? She does have a life back in Detroit. She's just finding herself. I asked her to make the sacrifice and spend time with me when I get back from Denver."

"And?"

"And, she needed to think about it. If she wanted to, she would say yes."

"She may want to. I'm sure that night meant as much to her as it did to you. Look, the Valencia thing was crap. She's like a lot of women who made a choice to follow her father's command as opposed to following her heart. It happens. That's the kind of life she grew up in. You knew that from the start. Her father had certain arrangements that he made without her knowledge. Count it joy that you got away from that family when you did. As for Keiko, I don't see her following anyone's rules for her life anymore. She's been through that. Perhaps, she wants a soft landing with you but you're both too stuck in where your lives are now to take the leap."

"Well, I'll see when I return. I sent her a text with the code to my apartment. If she's there when I return, I'll know that she wants to, at least, talk about it. If not, I'll have to come up with another plan. I want her, Callum. Make no doubt about that. I really thought that my heart wouldn't have room to fall in love with another woman."

"When did it happen?"

"Over a year ago. I had taken the team out for a celebratory dinner at my favorite restaurant back home. You already know which one I'm talking about. This was right after her divorce was final. Keiko handled all of the arrangements. At the end of the night, after everyone had gone home, she was dealing with the check with the manager since she keeps the company credit card with her. I stayed at the table enjoying a drink. I thought she had left. She came back and sat down. We talked for over two hours. We were there so long, pretty much closing down the place, that I had her double the payment on the bill for the night along with a massive tip for the four waiters who handled our tables. That wasn't our first time sitting down to talk like that. Something was different. She was different. It was right after the breakup with Valencia. I was still crushed over that. For those few hours, Valencia never came to mind. I realized there was more to Keiko. From that night, I started paying attention. Week after week, after week, I fell hard for her. Add in the intimacy we shared and it's a done deal. How do I get her to see that we can have something without it seeming out of place as if it's an office romance? It's not that at all."

Before they could continue, the phone on the plane rang. It had to be Tellum calling to be sure they were on their way to the meeting. He was still on his honeymoon but Byrum knew he wanted to be on the call.

"Does he know?" Callum asked, pointing to the phone.

"No. For now, it's still just you and me. Thanks for being an ear," Byrum said before answering the phone.

"Any and every time you need me, I'm here."

Keiko had to feel some of what he was feeling. If so, she'll be at his apartment when he got back. He was holding onto that. Next, he needed to find a way to have more with her. His desire was too strong to look the other way or to go back to them having only a working relationship. He was thinking of a different kind of relationship.

"Tell! Honeymoon over already?" Byrum asked when he finally answered the ringing phone. His mood was suddenly brighter.

"Y'all are crazy! Every day is a honeymoon with my wife!" Tellum exclaimed.

"I told him he had to say that," Cheyenne yelled from the background.

"Hey, sis!" Callum and Byrum said at the same time.

"Hey you two. I'm going to leave you to talk business. He only gets a few hours while I'm out shopping for some return home gifts for the family. Love you both!"

"Don't believe her. I wasn't under duress at all. Just under love. What's shaking?" Tellum asked. "Anything new?" he added.

Byrum looked to Callum. They were on the same page. For now, they would keep Tellum in the dark about what was going on between him and Keiko. The less people who knew, the better.

"We were looking over these latest financials and they are wowing us. Did you read them yet?" Byrum asked.

"I haven't. I only skimmed them. Cheyenne is not playing when she said no work. I take like an hour a day to catch up, but that's it. I saw what I needed to see. Most of all, I see big quarterly bonuses for the staff. When we win, they win also," Tellum declared.

"For sure. Let's talk about the meeting Callum and I are about to go into when we land. The season is about to jump off there in Denver in a few months. We want to be ready. We've booked Kendrick Lamar. His people confirmed with the office just last week. I got that good news while I was in Detroit. That's going to be big. The moment we announce it, the resort and surrounding hotels will fill up quickly. We need to be ready with extra permits and transportation. I hear he'll have SZA with him. It's going to be a great pull for that area and the resort."

"Callum, bring us up to speed since you negotiated the deal to get him to perform."

Byrum was happy for the reprieve once Callum took over the call. Taking out his cell phone, Byrum sent a text to Keiko. He didn't want to shy away from letting her know when she was on his mind. He was hoping the feeling was mutual. He sent three words and stared at his screen. He wasn't expecting a response. At this time, she was in the middle of new staff interviews. He just wanted her to know by keeping it short and sweet; *Thinking of you.*

He put his phone away and focused on the conversation around him. He needed to get back into work mode. He would hopefully find out, once he returned, if she was thinking the same way.

8

"That's the last of the interviews for today. I've noted our recommendations. It looks like everyone who was interviewed today will get a job offer. Going through the initial list of candidates before we conducted interviews helped cut the list down. That was a great idea. Do you want me to work on those letters to the selectees for you? I know it's getting pretty late."

Keiko smiled over at Sarai who sat on the other side of the desk with her three-tiered rolling laptop stand. On top was her laptop and a slot for both her iPad and her cell phone. The second shelf held folders and papers while the bottom shelf held a mobile printer. Everyone in the office had one that they could roll from one meeting to the other for convenience.

"Um, what? I'm sorry. I was a bit distracted," Keiko said and wished that she'd been paying attention. She'd been off all day.

"A bit distracted? You were focused during the interviews, but since I've been sitting here, there is clearly something else on your mind. Do you need me to repeat anything I just said?"

"No, I think I have it all."

Keiko looked down at the paper on her desk with the checkmarks next to all five names. Their interviews were superb.

"Are you sure? I know it's the end of the day and you told everyone to take an hour off early today to go do something relaxing. I don't mind hanging around if you need me to finish this up today."

"No, no. I meant what I said. You go ahead and head out. This can wait until tomorrow. I do want the job offers to go out within three days. You have some time. It's Friday night and I'm sure there is something you would rather be doing that isn't work related."

"Very true. What has you so happy these days? I mean, you're always smiling and happy, which makes working as your assistant easy. It's just that, since you came back from the wedding, you've been on cloud nine. Something has you extra, *extra* happy. Did you meet someone at the wedding? Are you holding out on me?" Sarai asked.

Keiko smiled and knew that she had nothing to share. That didn't keep her mind from going down memory lane. The only person she told about what happened was her bestie, Madison. Telling anyone else, especially someone around the office would never happen. She needed to protect, not only her image, but Byrum's as well.

"Really? I haven't noticed a difference. I did get to spend a lot of time with my son. I miss him so much. Thankfully, I get to travel home to see him anytime I want. I'm expecting to chat with his father about when Tru is coming here for the rest of the summer."

"You know, some people thought you had a daughter. I never clear them up because it's your personal business. You don't really share much about it other than with me when it comes to office staff. I want you to know that I take that to the heart."

"I've heard a few people reference me having a daughter. It's probably because my son has long black hair. He gets that from me. Every time we try to cut it, he gets crazy. I don't know how they could mistake him for a girl considering he dresses like a boy. All of the pictures in my office are of my son, not a daughter. I'm not the most open person when it comes to my personal life, so I get it. It's okay. They'll all get to meet him when he arrives. I'm going to bring him to the office. I didn't do that in Detroit because my life was in shambles when I started to work for the company."

"I understand. I have a daughter and I never bring her here. I was born and raised here on the island. I like to keep my life here at work separate from my life at home."

"Emmie, right? That's your daughter's name?"

Keiko hopes she got Sarai's daughter's name right.

"Yes. My dad's name is Emmett. My boyfriend and I named her after him with Emily; yes, we call her Emmie. Listen, a few of us girls are heading out for a girl's night out. The men on this island are friendly and sexy, though I'm not looking. If you're not seeing anyone, perhaps you might want to indulge? I know that when we're out and you're with us, you bring all the boys to the yard with your strikingly gorgeous exotic looks."

"I appreciate the compliment. I'll have to get back to you on that. I have some things to wrap up here. Text me the information on where you're going. I'll let you know if I can make it. I'm still kind of exhausted from my travels. I may just stay in, relax in a hot bubble bath, glass of wine in hand and a good book to read. I don't get to unravel often. Tonight seems like a good time to do it."

"That sounds like a good quiet night for you. If anyone deserves it, it's you. I marvel at how you keep everything in order around here. Byrum would be lost without you."

Many people have commented in the exact way since she began working for him. Keiko was finding herself lost without him since the night of the wedding. Hearing Sarai bring up his name reminded her that she had a choice to make tonight. Byrum would be returning in a few hours. She hadn't made up her mind on whether she was going to his place or not. Her body was screaming, yes! Her mind was still full of question marks.

For two days since he'd flown out to Denver once Callum picked him up in their jet, she had been reading over and over, the short text message he'd sent her. He'd sent a few others that were all work related to her work cell phone. To her personal one, the last text from him was the three words that she went to bed at night mulling over; *thinking of you*. He was on the plane when he sent that. She attempted to type a reply several times, but didn't. If she was going to think, she needed a clear head to do so. If she responded, it may have led to longer personal conversations. She wasn't ready for that yet.

"I appreciate you saying that. We are all a well-oiled machine. The entire team keeps us up and running smoothly."

Keiko looked up when there was a knock on her office door. It was Jalen, another one of the administrative team members.

"Keiko, I'm sorry to interrupt your meeting with Sarai. I'm heading out. I wanted you to know that there's a woman who has called a few times looking to speak to Byrum. You told us to never tell people when he was or was not on the island. She just called again. I didn't know if you wanted to handle that. I could also leave the messages for when Byrum returns."

Keiko knew who that was. For some reason, Valencia, his ex-girlfriend had been actively trying to reach Byrum for a few weeks. They had broken up over a year ago. Byrum was finally in a place where he was able to forget about what she'd done. Even though he hasn't moved onto another committed relationship, she knew that Valencia wouldn't be someone he would go back to; at least she hoped not. He didn't appear to be that gullible of a man. Valencia's actions had cut him deep.

"I'll take care of it in a few minutes," she replied.

"Do you want me to give you her number?" Jalen asked.

"No. I have it. She's called several times before and left her number. Have a good weekend, Jalen. You're doing great work," she noted.

As he often did, he saluted her. At first, people on the team didn't know what he meant when he did that. They've all come to realize that it was just his way of being kind and respectful. When she was young and living in Boston, there was a man named Sam in her neighborhood who would do that kind of salute along with a bow whenever he greeted someone. He would be seen with his dog everywhere he went. He would stop and do that salute and bow and then be on his way. People loved that and loved him. He was the kindest man she'd ever met. He was their community unacknowledged mayor. Jalen was that person for the office.

"I'm going to head out too, if you're sure you don't need me for anything else," Sarai said.

"Go and get out of here. I'll only be a few more minutes myself. I need to return that call Jalen just mentioned. After that, no more work for me either."

Sarai stood to leave.

"Don't forget to let me know if you are going to join us tonight. I understand if you don't. You can order room service now too. Since that started last month, the best winddown evening to have is when they deliver meals to the room and you don't have to leave out to pick anything up or take any dishes back unless you want to. Besides, the resort has the best food on the island. I can't wait for us to open and others get to taste the Mediterranean delicacies."

"I'm with you on that. I love those Greek lemon potatoes and those beef kabobs with the marinade made of balsamic vinegar, Worcestershire sauce, and Dijon mustard. I get that often. I'll be sure to let you know about tonight. Thanks for your help with the interviews. Byrum expects all of the new staff to be hired within the next few months. We still have plenty of interviews to get through. They'll be lots of training and tons of uniforms to order. We'll be slammed until the grand opening next summer. I hope you're ready."

"I am."

Keiko's personal cell phone pinged. It was her mother. She'll call her after returning Valencia's call. Though she hated the woman on-sight, simply because she'd hurt Byrum, she forced herself to put on her happy voice as she dialed Valencia's number using the office phone. She answered on the first ring.

"Byrum?" the soft, yet demanding voice on the other end said.

"No, this is his assistant, Keiko."

"Oh, yes. I've met you several times. How are you? It's been a long time."

Not long enough, Keiko said to herself.

"Yes, it has been. I understand that you've been trying to reach Byrum. I'm sorry but he's not available at the moment. He's away on business. I figured I would call to let you know so that your calls don't continue to go unanswered."

"I tried reaching him at the Detroit office and they said the same thing. I guess he spends a lot of time in the air. He doesn't answer my calls or texts to his cell anymore. I was hoping to catch him in one of the offices. Do you know when he'll be returning? That's a crazy question, of course you do. You keep up with his entire life."

"He should be back in the office late on Sunday and then all day starting Monday. Is there anything I can help you with? I know you've called a lot."

"No, I just need to talk to him about everything that's in the news about my personal life. In case you haven't heard anything, Byrum's name has come up a few times. The media knows that before my...well, marriage, he and I were an item."

Keiko had seen the stories. She was actually mesmerized by the events that unfolded in Valencia's personal life from her arranged-marriage husband getting another woman pregnant recently to also finding out that her he also liked men. That was evident from the secret video recordings of him with several men that were leaked to the media. Valencia was divorcing him. In the back of her mind, Keiko felt like Valencia wanted to rekindle her life with Byrum now that her marriage was ending.

"Yes. I saw the stories. I'm sorry this is happening to you. I will give Byrum a message that you called when he returns. I wish you the best."

Keiko actually meant that sentiment. She wanted to see all women win. What she didn't like was that any win could mean leaving someone in a losing situation. In this case, it was Byrum.

"Thank you. I hope he's well."

"He is. I'll let him know you wish him well."

When the call ended, Keiko let out a breath of frustration that she had to be nice to Valencia after what she'd done.

She had been working for Byrum for about six months when his relationship ended. She saw what it had done to him and how he pulled himself out of that and got back to life. That ideal made her remember something that she had promised herself; she needed to get back to life as well. Her decision was made.

First, she had to call her mother back. She wasn't looking forward to the conversation that had started the day before she left to come back to the island.

She and her mother had decided to do lunch together while her father took Tru to the aquarium. The conversation didn't end well.

"Hey, mom," she said the minute her mother answered the call. She was hoping for a much better outcome than the last time they'd talked.

"I've been waiting for you to call me back. I left you a message early this morning," her mother explained as she leaped right in on the defense for no reason at all.

Keiko huffed silently so that she got the effect of the action but her mother didn't hear it to avoid a blowup from her.

"I know. I'm just getting back and there has been a lot going on heading into the weekend. I was going to call you earlier but ended up in another meeting."

"You do so much for that company and for the Blackstones in general. I hope they compensate you well. You're more than an assistant.'

Byrum crossed her mind when her thoughts turned to how much more she was for him than just his assistant; at least she was for that one night.

"I am paid very well. Besides my salary, all of my expenses are paid here and when I travel. They also cover a huge portion of my Detroit expenses. I couldn't ask for a better job. I'm learning a lot about business. You know I want to start my own virtual assistant business. I'm hoping to employ hundreds of assistants around the world to work virtually for companies. What I'm learning here will go a long way."

"Oh? You'll be even busier than you are now if on top of your current job, you start your own business. What about Tru? What about what we talked about when it comes to DeConnor? You know he's sorry for stepping out on you in your marriage. I'm sure whatever it was that you did to make him do that can be fixed. I still hope you will reconsider this divorce thing and get back together with him. You wouldn't have to work. He makes enough money to take care of his family like a man should. You shouldn't have to work this hard. Tru needs his mother around the clock. You could stay at home with him all the time."

Here they go again, Keiko thought. They were about to have a conversation that wasn't going to turn out well. She didn't know how much more she needed to say to convince her mother that her life with DeConnor was over and done with. Once she discovered his penchant for meeting women on internet dating sites as if, at that time, he was a single man, she was done. When the rest came out during the divorce, she was disgusted. Nothing would make her go back to the way he treated her.

"It's never going to happen. I am happy now, mom. I love my life. DeConnor and I co-parent well. Tru will be coming here soon to spend the summer with me. We'll have a lot of fun. I may not parent the way you did, but I'm still parenting.

Tru is a very happy and well-adjusted child to this new normal that is our life. I wouldn't want him to see me back with his father just because. I would be miserable. I don't want that for my son. I don't want to keep having this conversation with you if this is all you're going to keep calling me about. I want you and daddy to accept that I'm happy now. I wasn't happy with DeConnor. We really were not happy together. There were too many outside forces that pulled us apart. We were not a happy couple. He and I are done. Please let that go," she pleaded.

When her mother didn't respond on the other end, Keiko had a feeling that she was working up to trying to convince her that her life was back with her ex-husband; giving it an even bigger push that she ever has. She prepared herself for the fight by leaning back in her office chair, crossing an arm over her face to cover her eyes. The broken record of the story of her life with her ex was beyond getting old; it was ancient, dead, buried and now stinking. Her brain screamed, enough already.

"Okay. I hear you. I understand. I hope you can come visit us in Boston soon."

Surprise, surprise she thought and shot straight up in her chair. Her mother was clearly backing off.

"I promise I will. Tru and I will visit when he comes here. I love you, mom. I just want to live my life my way for a change. It already feels good. I plan to focus my attention on my son. He deserves to have two parents who are happy; not just one."

"I can tell that you are happier than you have been in a very long time."

"That's because I am. I'll call you in a few days. It's getting late and I need to get out of here. Tell dad I love him and I love you. We'll talk soon, okay?"

"Yes. That's perfect. Can I just say one more thing?" her mother asked.

Keiko braced herself for more of the same. She wanted her mother to speak her peace as long as she got the chance to counter with a little bit of peace of her own.

"Yes."

"If not with DeConnor, I hope that you find love again. It's good for the mind, body and soul. I know you're happy right now. I hope to see you even happier. Is that okay to say?"

She was shocked once again. Just when she pegged her mother for one personality, she displays a different one. Her mother surprised her after months of pushing DeConnor at her. She smiled and relaxed her body.

"Yes, that's perfect. I hope that for myself as well. I'll call you in a week," she said.

"I look forward it to it."

When the call ended, Keiko gathered everything up that she needed to take with her. She turned the light out and locked her office door. Racing to the elevator, her private cell rang again. She huffed in frustration that she was never going to get out of the office. Madison's face graced the screen. As she waited for the elevator, she answered.

"Hey, bestie!" she chimed happily into the phone.

"Hey. I won't keep you long. I'm hoping you're on your way to Byrum's place. That's a conversation for another day. I wanted you to know that I was able to carve out some time to visit you. I'm working on the new schedule for the nurses. I'm putting in for a week off. Can I still stay with you or should I get a hotel room since guest rooms on the resort aren't available for months yet?"

"Yes!" Keiko cheered. She hopped into the elevator when the doors opened. "You can, of course, stay with me. I can't believe you're finally coming. I can show you all around this place. Some areas we can't go into yet because of the active construction, but there is a lot to see and do around the island. Send me the dates so that I can carve out some days off while you're here. Like you, as head nurse, I have to make sure I have coverage, especially when it comes to what Byrum needs."

"Haha, some of his needs you can't field out though, right?" Madison jested.

"Real funny. I haven't been doing any of that...yet."

"Yet? I heard that. You decided?"

"I have. I was on my way to pack an overnight bag when you called."

Keiko tapped her foot impatiently now that she'd chosen being with Byrum tonight. For once, the elevator seemed to be moving very slow even though it only had to go down two levels.

"Oh, don't let me hold you up from your man."

"He's not my man, Madison."

"Oh, yes, he is. I see you in your future and trust me, you are with that man on a more permanent basis. It begins tonight when he gets home and finds you in his place in something hot and barely-there. That sexy stuff you like to buy should work. You buy the sexiest, steamiest stuff for someone who declares to not have a man."

"I buy them for me, not for a man. Though, I must say, I'm imagining modeling them all for Byrum."

"You sure would have enough of them, that's for sure."

"That and then some. I don't know why I didn't just say

yes when he first asked me to spend this time with him. It's not like we haven't already had sex; amazing sex; earth moving sex. I've been dying to be with him since I got back. I'm holding off on all self-pleasure orgasms. I need my strength and energy for what he brings to the table again and again and again..."

"I get it. The man gives you multiple orgasms for the first time in your life. I still can't believe DeConnor never did. Selfish bastard."

Keiko chuckled. She always got a good laugh from her best friend who was more pissed about what DeConnor didn't do sexually, yet he was out slinging that thing around with all kinds of women. She was just happy to know that he never did anything outside of their marriage without a condom. Still, after months and months of checking, she was clean and clear.

"Well, Byrum is far from a selfish lover. The way he made that night all about me still has me shivering at the thought of how he made me feel. Thinking back on it has kept me wide awake some nights."

"I'm hearing you will get your fill of all that unselfishness tonight. Have fun. I swear, I am so happy for you. I'm going to text you the dates for my visit. Make sure they line up with time you can get off. I want to burn the candle at both ends the whole time I'm there. I want to do so many devious things that when I return home, people will be able to see the visible word, 'shame' written on my forehead after all of the debauchery I can't wait to get into."

"That's for sure. I'm on board for that for you only because I know you could use a, let your hair down, moment. We're going to have a lot of fun. I know all the places I want us to check out while you're here. I promise, you will have a great time. I'll call you in a few days?" Keiko asked. "Does that work?"

"Yes, and you better. Tell Byrum, what's up. You won't but one day when I say that, you will. I know we're still being secretive. You know I always keep your secrets. This thing with Byrum is a good one."

"One day. Depending on the direction this thing with him goes in, I will let you know when you can shout it to the mountains. For now, mums the word, right?"

"Girl scouts honor," Madison shouted playfully.

"Girl, neither of us were girl scout's but I appreciate the sentiment. Anyway, I need to get moving. Wish me luck?" Keiko questioned.

"You don't need it. You are beautiful and that man only has eyes for you. I wish, hope and pray that a man will one day look at me the way he looks at you. Even before all this sex the two of you had, I remember being at your company events and seeing how he ogled you from afar. That man couldn't wait to get between them creamy thighs of yours. Now that he has, he's going to sit a spell for the pleasure for you both. Eat it all up."

"Trust me, I'm all over it. Be safe and we'll talk soon," Keiko said and ended the call.

She quickly sent a text to Sarai to let her know that she was going to pass on the outing tonight with the ladies. She had a man to go see after going to her place to shower and change. No more hesitation with Byrum. She's waited too long to be on his radar. Now that she was, this was her time.

9

Byrum made his way through customs and headed for the car that should be waiting for him at the airport to take him home. The almost ten-hour flight was exhausting. Still, he felt a new vigor at the thought of what he may find when he got home. He could have easily found out Keiko's decision by calling her, but he decided to let the mystery live in the air until he got to his place. That way, he wouldn't be disappointed on the ride there. He took a call from his father who was calling just as he handed his overnight bag to his driver.

"Pop! How is Los Angeles treating you?"

"It's good, son. Your mother is also having the time of her life. We're going to a show at the Hollywood Bowl tonight. The plan, right now, is to stay a few extra days, unless one of you need me back in Detroit."

Byrum thought about the happiness his parents showed that was possible to him and his brothers every day. He knew things hadn't always been perfect, but he loves that even during any times that brought about a struggle, they did it together. He loved their love. Perhaps that's why he, Tellum and Callum were more particular about love than men their ages. Knowing they were doing what they had always planned to do, which was to spend more quality time together in their later years, he wouldn't dare interrupt that with anything related to business back at home. None of them were there, so business will wait.

"No, enjoy your time away with mom. You both deserve this time. You've worked a lot of years to have this time with her, even though you're still working."

"Ah, but the truth is, I'm pretty much working with my sons and for myself. Everything about this time in my life is perfect, including joining forces with my three favorite sons."

Byrum chuckled loudly.

"Unless you think I don't know, we are your only favorite sons!" he laughed.

"Ah, you caught that! Listen, I can plan out my day without a lot of hassle these days. This is the life. I can continue to build something with my sons while also making sure the love of my life wakes up pleased with each day. Remind me when we're all in Detroit or at least when we have some time to connect, your mother wants to talk about starting that foundation in Hawaii."

Byrum brightened at the thought that his mother was joining them in not just creating a new resort, but to also give back to the people of Hawaii by starting a foundation that would aid in the education of the island's youth.

"She's really about that, huh? I knew she was serious about the foundation the moment we shared with both of you that we acquired the location in Hawaii. Mom told all of us to not just focus on building more wealth but to make sure the people who live on the islands we choose can see and feel that we care by putting money back into them. I love that she wants to do that. Tellum said Cheyenne wants to be a part of the team."

"Son, this will truly be a family affair. One day when you and Callum marry incredible women, because I know you will,

I hope they'll take part in the cause."

Byrum opened his mouth to push that narrative of marriage for him out of the narrative when an image of a beautiful, smiling Keiko filled his head. His head and heart swooned with the thought of her. Why was he thinking of her when his father uttered the word, marriage? He shook off the thought.

"Speak that to Callum. I'm pleading the fifth," he noted and made light of.

"If you say so. Nothing makes me happier than being in business with my sons while being able to do that on my own time. I love it. Your mom loves it more than me. She's always wanted to be a bigger part in what you boys are building. She's put a lot of time and effort into what to do for the people of Hawaii. She's secretly formed her own team and they've been meeting a few times a month via Zoom. She's excited to share her plan. I told her that I would bankroll any idea she has."

"Pop, you know your sons got her and you when it comes to anything financial. We know you have it. As I know Tellum and Callum constantly reiterate for you, this is our time to give back to you and mom for all that we are. Any bankrolling for anything she or you want to put into play, we got you."

"I know, I know. I told her that, as well. She told me that because of her husband who taught her sons well when it came to building wealth and not just making money, she wasn't concerned about where the money would come from. The three of you continue to make us happy. This foundation, with its start in Hawaii will eventually expand to all of your resort locations. That's the legacy she wants to leave so that someday, our grandchildren and great-grandchildren will be reminded of how important it is to give back. More about that soon. I do have one other thing to chat about if you have a few more minutes."

"Of course, I do. What's up, Pop?"

"I wanted you to know that I went over the contract with the new law firm out of New York. They are opening up their Detroit office and we're their first clients in town."

"That's great. You and Tellum worked out a hell of a deal, Pop. I love that this firm is black-owned."

"I agree. They are Jarreau, Gerard and Associates. Our personal attorney is Adrian Jarreau. I've known his father, David and his former partner, Armand Gerard for many years. Armand's son, Zacarious and Adrian have taken over the reins of the firm. David and Armand had a contract with General Motors when I worked there. I believe that also passed down to the sons. They are doing big things by taking the firm in a new and improved direction by opening up offices in other states. They deal a lot in artificial intelligence cases. Tellum liked him right off the bat. I know you boys will be dealing with AI and I thought they would be a good fit. Turns out that they are perfect. Tellum went to New York and took a tour of their New York office. He was able to meet with the team who will be working with us. Adrian assured us that one of the partners will always be available to us whenever we need them. He told us to always start with him since he's the managing partner. If he's tied up, which he will be I'm sure, someone else will be ready at a moment's notice to handle any issues we have. He will remain in the New York office but he assured us that we'll get the same care from the team he's setting up in Detroit. His plan is to work with us as directly as possible; his preference. He loves what you boys are creating and building. With the expansion of the business, we needed a new law firm. Tellum was centered on this one. He says they also represent Duron Knight's architecture firm out of Atlanta along with their Los Angeles and Boston offices. I love seeing y'all young folks doing the damn thing."

Byrum put the peace sign up in the air. He enjoyed all the progress they were making. They agreed, that as brothers in business together, they would never settle for where they were as long as there was room to grow.

"Thanks, Pop. You taught us well. We appreciate your help and guidance along the way. Listen, are you still going to meet with the Detroit executive team when you get back home? I may be a while getting back. Tellum is still on his honeymoon and I think Callum is trying to connect with Kendra before the basketball season heats up for her."

"I can do that. I spoke with Callum before I called you. He told me he would only be in Detroit briefly before heading to her home in Las Vegas to see her. Are they serious? They've been together a little minute now. That's odd for him, just like it is for you. Your mother seems to think that you'll be next to fall in love and get married after Tellum."

"Pop, you know me better than that."

"Hey, I know. I pay attention to what you say and declare. I've been telling her that, but she insists that she knows her sons better than I do."

"That's because she does when it comes to matters of the heart. She believes she knows us better than we know ourselves."

"That's because I do."

Byrum chuckled hearing his mother chime in, in the background. Felicia Blackstone never missed a chance to speak her mind. Byrum shook his head at her assumption that she knows him better than he even knows himself.

"Hey, mom," he said as his driver weaved his way through the heavy evening traffic. It was only eight in the evening but it was a Friday night. The island would be hopping with its exciting night-life.

"Hey, son. Have you landed back on the island?" she asked.

"I just did. I'm headed to my apartment."

"Okay. Is Keiko back yet?"

He knew it. Byrum knew that it would only be seconds before his mother found a way to bring Keiko into the conversation. He loved her but he had to continue keeping anything about his private life a secret. He didn't want to give her false hope when he still wasn't clear about what would come out of his time with Keiko after the wedding.

"You're asking me about Keiko?" Byrum questioned.

"Felicia?"

Byrum heard his father call his mother up on her knack for being intrusive into her son's personal lives; this time, his.

"What? I like her. I'm just hoping she made it back safe. I didn't get to talk to her at the end of the reception."

"That's because you and Pop snuck off. I didn't forget," Byrum boasted laughingly.

"Blame that on your father. Keiko?" she asked again.

It was clear his mother wasn't going to let the subject go.

"Yes. She made it back safely and is back to work."

"She sure is beautiful, don't you think, Byrum?"

"Felicia, stop it right now," Dennis said.

"It's okay, Pop. Yes, she is beautiful. She always has been. I was surprised to see her at the wedding. You didn't make sure Cheyenne invited anyone else from my team. Is there a reason why that you'd like to share with me?" Byrum asked.

His mother cleared her throat. He was putting her on the spot. She didn't like when that happened, though she loved putting all of them on the spot.

"No reason at all. I have to run. It's eleven in the morning here and I have a lot I want to do today. Make sure you tell Keiko that I said hello and that I hope to see her again real soon. I love you, son."

"Love you too, mom."

There was a pause before his father spoke up. No doubt, he was waiting to be alone.

"She's obvious, isn't she?" Dennis asked.

"I could drive a plane through how open and obvious she is. That's mom."

"Any truth to what she's insinuating?"

Byrum didn't usually offer up information that wasn't asked of him. Now that his father is asking, he didn't want to lie. He and his brothers were always up front with their father. If they asked him to keep a secret, even from their mother, he did. They would never ask him to keep anything bad from her, but man to man, they were able to count on their father to come at them straight. He was about to do that with him.

"Yes. Can you not tell mom? I can't handle talking to her about Keiko yet when I don't even know where things are leading."

"Your secret is safe with me. I hate that she's always right about these things. She was right about Tellum and Cheyenne. It looks like she's right about you and Keiko. Don't be mad at her if she butts in some more. It's her thing. She wants more daughters and of course, it goes without saying, but I will say it, she wants a heap of grandchildren. You can't fault her for wanting that now that life is slowing down. She's ready to enjoy playing with and watching her grandchildren. Of course, she wants all three of you married. She's already hoping Cheyenne will be pregnant sooner rather than later."

"It's fine, Pop. If I know Tellum, trust me, babies will be popping out from the two of them real soon. As for me, not so much. I love mom more than anything in this world. She means well. She's still worried about what happened with Valencia. I keep trying to assure her that I'm fine. I promise you I am."

"I don't think your mother saw much of a future for you with Valencia. She never spoke about seeing a future for the two of you; not like she's already claiming for you and Keiko. Like you said, she means well. Anyway, the contract with the law firm is good. You'll each need to review the documents and sign them. You can do that through Docusign to make it easier to do since it's hard to catch the three of you in the same place to sign."

"Sounds good. I'll be on the lookout for that."

"Enjoy your time with Keiko tonight."

Byrum looked at his phone and shook his head. How his father knew, he had no clue.

"Don't try to figure me out. I just know."

"In that case, I'm on it. Look, my car just pulled up to my place. If we're good, I'll talk to you in a few days. I think in a few weeks, all three of us will be in Detroit at the same time. We'll have to do a guys' night out since the chance to hang like that are few and far in between."

"I look forward to that. Listen, when it comes to Keiko, don't allow your past to play any part in what you may have with her. She deserves to get all of you, all of your heart, if that's the direction you really want to go in. I have to side with your mother, that she's a good woman. I think she'll be good for you."

Byrum exited the car as his driver got his bag. He tried to look up to the top floor apartment as if he could see any signs that Keiko was in there. He wouldn't know until he got inside."

"I hear you. I'm on it. Believe me, when I know, I'll make sure you and mom both know. Later, Pop."

"Later, son. I love you," Dennis said.

Byrum smiled. His father never hesitated in sharing his love for his sons in his actions and most of all, in his words.

"I love you too, Pop."

Byrum tipped his driver handsomely, as he always does. He then raced under the long running awning and inside of his building. It had begun to rain as soon as they left the airport. It wasn't a downpour, but he was still appreciative of the awning.

He stopped at the front desk to retrieve his mail. It wasn't often that building security kept track of mail and packages that arrived for residents. He paid extra for the service knowing that he would sometimes be gone for more than a week. His mail would sometimes pile up too high to fit in his mailbox. Even though Keiko would sometimes come by to get his mail if he was away for more than a few days, he didn't want to burden her with that task knowing she had enough to hold down at the office.

"Welcome home, Mr. Blackstone. It's only been a few days but you have a lot of mail in that short period of time. I was going to give it to your assistant when she arrived, but her hands were already full. I told her I would hold it for when she came back down. She didn't say anything as she walked off.

Looks like you arrived before she left back out."

Byrum stood stoic, his one eyebrow raised in question. He couldn't move. He wasn't sure he'd heard him.

"Uh, Dimitri, did you say my assistant is here? Keiko was here and is still here?"

"Yes. Miss Keiko arrived about an hour ago. She said you gave her the code to your apartment, so I let her up. She already had the code to the elevator. I hope that was okay."

Byrum felt like a giddy kid in elementary school knowing that the prettiest girl in his class liked him. Unlike some boys who acted like they hated girls at that age, he was all over trying to woo the prettiest one in pigtails. Excited that he got his wish for the night, he reached into his pocket and gave Dimitri an enormous tip of the few hundred dollars he had on him. Getting the news was well worth the extra tip.

"You have no idea how perfect that decision was," he smiled, handing it over.

Byrum was suddenly ready to end the conversation. He felt like superman. Like the superhero, he wanted to leap the building in a single jump. That's how excited he was.

Dimitri looked at the many large bills in wonder. He looked from the money over to Byrum.

"Sir?" Dimitri questioned.

Though he often tipped him handsomely at the end of each week, this extra he knew meant something as was the intent.

"Have a good night, Dimitri. I appreciate you," Byrum said after gathering his stack of mail before waving and rushing to the elevator.

"Yes, sir. It's a fantastic evening in deed," Dimitri hollered at his back. Byrum turned just as he got to the elevator and caught Dimitri doing a happy dance.

He wanted to dance himself.

As he waited, he heard Dimitri making a phone call.

"Baby, tomorrow night, we are going out on the town since it's my day off. Get your prettiest dress out and see if your mother can watch the kids. We are about to paint the town red!" Dimitri excitedly said into the phone.

Stepping inside of the elevator, as it moved, it seemed to take longer than usual to reach his floor. He laughed at himself when he noticed he was tapping his foot as if the elevator was going slower than usual; it wasn't. When it finally did stop and he got out, Byrum's long strides excited him. Using his code for the keypad at the door, it opened and to his delight, there she was. Like something out of a dream, Keiko looked up from the sofa where she was lounging and watching an old movie and just like that, he fell in love. It took him a moment to realize exactly what his mother saw in them and what he now knew he wanted with her. Keiko has always been beautiful and sexy. In his space, she was now a vision of the future. He could imagine coming home all the time and finding her just like this.

"You're really here," he said, a hint of surprise in his voice. It was also the sound of the world's happiest man walking.

"Yes, I am happily here."

Byrum couldn't move once he closed the door and locked it.

"You are the best sight in this entire world. Come here, baby," he said on a sexy whisper with three words completely filled with love.

When Keiko jumped up and raced to him, he dropped his bag and the mail to the floor, not caring about any of it as the mail fluttered out all around his feet. He stepped on and over it to get to her. All he wanted was to feel her in his arms. He was a desperate man who desperately wanted nothing but her; to see her; to feel her; to kiss her and most of all, to love all on her. Keiko didn't disappoint his desire for her. In her short, white nightie, he braced his feet for her leap and caught her by gripping her bare behind and pulling her intimately close to him. Her skin was hot to the touch. She was soft and all things gorgeously woman. He was reminded of the nights he'd thought about her being in his arms like this even before that night after the wedding. He did remember that his visions of her during times of his solo showers were how he reached a self-pleasuring orgasm in mere minutes. Actually, being inside of her was so much better than his hot dreams of her.

Before he could get a word out, Keiko planted the sexiest, most welcoming kiss on his lips. God, he loved her, he thought before his mind went blank of anything else other than the feel of her.

The tender moment went on and on as they feasted on each other as if he'd been away at war, returning with a new zest for life and for her. He focused on exploring her mouth with his tongue, stroking hers with the same ferocious need that she was planting on him. With her arms around his neck, she bounced in his arms as if she couldn't seem to get close enough to his body. He understood; it was how he was feeling. All he knew was that she was putting her trust in him, in them, and he wouldn't take it for granted. She didn't have to be here tonight just because he asked. He wanted her to want to be with him as much as he wanted and needed to be with her. Knowing the feeling was mutual was life altering for him. He would think about how later. Right now, he wanted to feel.

Reliving their night together in his head had plagued him, especially when he thought that he'd never hold her like this again. He was ecstatic knowing that she had the ability to turn his frown into an instantaneous great big smile.

Pulling back for a second, he went at her mouth again, tasting and parting her lips with his tongue to get more of her essence, her smell, her sweet taste. She tasted as sweet as the sweetest fruit. Her taste enchanted him.

"You smell delicious," he finally said, still holding her.

Byrum growled out his pleasure against her lips.

"I've been waiting for you," Keiko slurred out sexily.

"Oh? That's a good thing. I was hoping for exactly that."

"I know you were. I'm sorry if I gave you cause to think I wouldn't be here. It wasn't easy, trust me. After all, this is you. There is so much at stake."

Byrum put her down on her feet and took her by the hand as he walked into the bedroom. As much as he wanted to talk, the idea of what he really wanted to do took over. He didn't want to hesitate and proving that she made the right choice in being here tonight. The plan was to make sure this wasn't the only night. He needed to get out of his clothes so that he could shower before enjoying a quiet night alone with her. He didn't want to stop their conversation. He just wanted to keep moving toward getting him and her naked. There was no doubt that he wanted much more than joining their bodies and sinking into the depths of her womanhood. His mind had been on her so much that first, intimacy was what he wanted for them and not just for him.

"At stake? Like what? Did something happen?" he asked.

He couldn't any doubt. If there was some, he wanted to rid their space of it.

"Well, Sarai mentioned that the team was going to hang out tonight. They invited me. I decided that I would rather be here with you. I know I wouldn't be able to stop beating myself up if you came back and I wasn't here. It wasn't just about you but about me knowing I wanted to be here more than anything else. It wouldn't have been my best night out with them. I gave her a story that I was going to relax in my room by taking a hot bath, drinking some wine and stuff. I texted to let her know I would take a raincheck. I went back to my place to get ready and then I headed out. That's when it happened."

Byrum looked to her face to see if what happened may have been something really bad that would show up on her face. He didn't see anything horrific. She did look worried when he watched her lips curve right before she began nibbling on the lower lip. Even though this wasn't the moment to get even more aroused, watching her lips did just that. He tamed his desire and focused on what was bothering her.

"What? Tell me what happened," he said, cautiously and caring.

Byrum began removing his shoes and clothes as if doing so in her presence was a natural thing. They had only been together once, but he felt like being with Keiko was exactly how naturally it was supposed to be.

"Well, I called a rideshare to bring me here. I had my overnight bag over my shoulder. It's the same one the team has seen me use when I'm heading home for a few days. I was getting in the car when Sarai walked out of the resort through the side entrance. I thought I was avoiding everyone by using that door. I was specific to the rideshare to not use the main entrance but to come around to the side. When she saw me with my bag, I saw all kinds of questions on her face. She kept looking from my face to my bag. She knew I wasn't leaving the island to go back to Detroit or the team would have been made aware. I had to be quick on my feet. I told her I was going to spend the night at one of our competitor resorts to see how their services were. I said I wanted to make sure the training of our new staff was top-tier if I could check out how another resort and their staff treated guests. I heard my voice shaking as I tried to explain that I could only figure some of that out by checking out other places. For a few seconds, she just stood there as if she was thinking through whether what I said was the truth or not. Then she said that it was a good idea and that I would still get to enjoy my night in. Then she checked her phone and told me to let her know how my stay was when she came in on Monday. That was close. I thought I would be tongue-tied. She seemed to take that explanation in stride."

Bryum heard her blow out a breath of relief that hopefully that story worked. He wanted her to not give it another thought. He knows what any revelation about her true intent could mean for them. At this point, he didn't care. If what he was feeling for her was matched by her feelings for him, they would make it through unscathed. He would see to that. What Keiko meant to him outweighed any gossip heard from the staff.

"Baby, the only tongue-tied moments you should have are with me, like we just shared. That kiss gave me life. You have no idea how much I longed for that. As for Sarai and anyone else on the team, I hope they are focused on their own lives and not what is happening with yours or mine or ours together. I want you to relax and not worry. We are not making history as the first office romance," he explained, removing the rest of his clothing.

He looked up and found Keiko looking at him with a side-eye.

"Office romance? Is that what this is?"

"No, but it will be what people think. You should know me by now. I don't give a damn what anyone thinks other than you. I will take care of you and your image. People need to know that what happens between two consenting adults in any arena is between that man and that woman. In this case, you and me. Now, can we focus on us and not anyone else? This time together will be short enough; much shorter than I'd like. For now, I'll take what I can get. I'm glad you're here. You are sexy as hell," he noted, taking in every part of her.

Naked, he stood and reached for her. Kissing her soulless again, he reached down and pulled her nightie from her body before sliding her thin, silky white panties down her legs. Byrum didn't miss the chance to inhale her essence as he leaned down and then slowly rose back up.

"They tied at the hip," Keiko exclaimed on a shriek when his hand slid slowly up her body and was planted between her legs. When he moved his fingers in a circular motion, meant to have her mind on feeling and nothing else, she gasped delightedly and grabbed onto his arms to keep from collapsing in a heap on the floor in front of him.

"I'll remember that for another time, perhaps involving my teeth. Sorry, but I needed to feel you. I've been thinking about doing so since that night. Shower with me."

"Byrum, I've already showered. I wanted to be ready for you when you got here."

He wiggled his finger at her to let her know that's not what he was talking about.

"See, I wasn't really planning on us actually showering. Do

you have any idea of the torture I've been in seeing you around the office when all I wanted to do was grip this perfect ass of yours in my hands? My mouth has been watering nonstop thinking about taking your breasts into my mouth, getting as much pleasure from that as I want to give you. I have been hungering for your sweet feel and even more for your sweet taste."

Keiko winked at him as she moved her hands up and down his arms.

"I bought dinner over with me," she explained.

"You already know that's not the taste I'm hungry for, but I get your desire to be playful. I love it. We can eat later; and I plan to with food and other parts of you. Shower?"

Keiko winked again.

"Up," was all she said.

Byrum picked her up into his arms and walked into the adjoining bathroom. He took no time in opening the shower door to turn on the water. While they waited for it to heat up, he tasted her mouth again.

"We have a lot to talk about. I think that one night and this night aren't it for me," he quickly shared.

Byrum didn't care what it would take. He wanted them to belong to each other.

"Me either. I know that now. I was willing to live on that hill of one night with you until I saw you back at the office. I knew that my craving, my desire for you wasn't over. I don't know what will happen, but I agree, we should talk about it."

When he saw steam from the shower, he kissed her sweetly one last time before walking them inside of it.

He turned to place her back against the wall the furthest away from the hot water. As it cascaded over his body, he cupped water and rained some down over her, starting with her hair.

"Mmm, that feels good," she said.

"I love the new haircut," he said close to her ear, where he kissed all around it. He loved that the water flowed down his body and onto hers, wetting her body, especially her hard, pebbled nipples. Seeing her desire continued to stoke his need for her without much effort. Everything about her kept him in a state of arousal.

"You noticed?"

Byrum turned his lips up in disbelief that she thought he didn't see all of her at all times; even the slightest change like a new hair style.

"Sweetheart, I notice everything about you including the fact that your toes are no longer green with glitter on them but they're now hot pink. So are your fingernails."

Keiko raised up and kissed his cheek.

"You see me," she slurred out when his hand slipped down between them to play in the moisture he found between her legs. It wasn't from the water coming from the shower. It was from her own sexy core.

Byrum could smell her sweet scent of arousal. He felt her body respond to his slight touch.

"I also feel you. Do you feel me?" he quietly asked against her thoroughly kissed lips.

"Yes," she moaned.

"What do you feel?"

Keiko moaned again after he moved his body from left to right against hers, allowing her to feel what the idea of her did to him.

"You're hard; very hard."

"I love how you are not shy about saying that. Never be shy around me. When we are together, what happens and is said between us is for us to share. That can mean a simple conversation to the hottest, steamiest of sexy connotations."

"I won't."

Byrum didn't want to talk anymore. They'd done enough of that already. He wanted to get down to what he's been missing; being inside of her.

He reached behind her to the rack with his shower gel on it. He retrieved the condom he'd placed there before he left for his trip. He'd bought extra and had them in various places around his apartment. He was keeping hope alive that she would be here. She was the first woman to enter his space. His thoughts were on her when he bought them. He was a man who loved women and so condoms were a normalcy in his life. Here on the island, they were for her only. He raised the condom up and showed it to her.

"Before you question why this is here, I put them in a few places around the apartment just in case you were going to be here. I don't want to have to take the time to race around to grab one if we desire to take each other in any part of this apartment. This wasn't conveniently placed here for anyone else but you."

"I wasn't wondering but thanks for telling me. I am happy that you did. I don't know if I want to wait for you to go get one and come back. Besides, knowing a man's desires isn't foreign to me. Don't forget I've known you for quite a while. I know…"

Byrum placed his finger against her lips. He didn't want her to share what he knew was about to come from her lips.

"Since I've been here on the island, I haven't been with

anyone. Not even before we connected at the wedding. I've been too busy thinking about work and wondering how I could convince you that I wanted you. I know what you were about to say. It was probably something about me and other women. I'm not choir boy, but when I say I've wanted you and only you, I mean that."

Keiko looked down and then back up at him.

"I like your version of wanting me."

Byrum moved his hand a little faster between her legs, enjoying the feel of her nails as they dug into his arms. Seeing Keiko this aroused had him wanting to get through the work of getting protection in place.

"Baby, you give new meaning to slippery when wet," he said, stressing that last word by prolonging it on his tongue. He proved that by letting his tongue slip out, rolling it across her waiting lips.

After putting the condom in place, Byrum pressed her against the wall. He kissed her lips, then her nose, before making his way to her forehead. He moved his head around to her neck as the water covered them completely. Their heavy breathing was an aphrodisiac.

He moved his hands down to her bare hips, where he stroked both sides from there to the top of her knees. He could feel her fingers stroking his back. He ground his body against hers in a slow dance that generated more heat than the hot water of the shower. He lifted her up slowly.

With her legs curved around him, he gently and easily slid inside of her. With a slow rhythm playing in his head, he moved to it with his hips not rushing, no hurry of the moment. He wanted to feel her and have her feel him. Their first time, he didn't rush but he tried to get in everything he was feeling for her with every stroke. Now, he was less focused on the stroke and more on being in the moment with her.

They loved like that, him pushing forward and up into her while she moved her hips in tangent with his. He kept his hands on the curve of her hips while the wall behind her gave them the leverage they needed.

The kissing was powerful. It held meaning in the slow way in which their mouths loved each other. A few minutes passed by when he placed her feet down on the shower floor.

He kissed her passionately, not breaking the sensual connection of their mouths as he turned her body around so that her back was to him. He placed her hands flat against the marble wall. She parted her legs and accepted his love from behind with the eloquent grind into her body. The loving was still gradual and precise. His movements brought out the love he was feeling for her. He felt it flowing from her to him. They loved like this with her hands braced on the wall while one of his hands played in her hair. The other stayed possessively on her hips.

Byrum leaned back and watched her body move back into his, enjoying the feel of not just sex, but what he now knew was true love. He'd been in love with her for months. He was hoping he'd never have to go backwards from their time together. Seeing them together in his future was all he wanted now. He kissed her back and her neck, licking a wet path across her back. His body was unable to even think of stopping the pleasurable interlocking. He knew he never wanted to lose this feeling.

In yet, another move, he moved from her body and turned so that he was seated on the white marble seat in the shower. No words were spoken. They talked only with their eyes and their bodies. He guided Keiko to face him in a sitting motion on his lap. She slid her body down over his; her mouth forming the perfect, 'O'. He held her up while she took control of their loving.

As Keiko bounced slowly up and down, he knew that her release wasn't far; neither was his. When she moved slightly faster, throwing her head back, he moved his hands up to her back and gyrated his hips to enhance their equal pleasure. When Keiko finally let go and dwelled in the fast acting, vibrancy of her release, he enjoyed the howling sound of her orgasm taking all of her over.

He captured her breast in his mouth and sucked as his own release gripped him in a choke hold. He growled as an orgasm more powerful than he thought was humanly possible cascaded all around and through him, his surging pumps fiercer and more precise as he loved her with all that was in him. They rode out the idyllic escalading passion together.

The shower water poured over them as they remained in this position of him holding her tight in his arms. They would talk, he knew. That wasn't possible right now. His head was exploding with white lightning-force desire. This wasn't the time for talking; he only wanted to feel and love. Desire on a whole new level was the current state of his heart as it beat rapidly in his chest. This time was meant for them to take in what they just shared. Though he loved all things sex, he needed this slow lovemaking with Keiko tonight. His heart was involved. Tonight was different. He was, for the second time in his life, deeply in love. Keiko was it for him. No way would he be able to share this kind of desire with another woman. He never wanted to. He loved her and only her.

Byrum pulled her closer to his body as she slid down on it

more comfortably.

"Baby, thanks for making my night. I'm not talking about the explosive sex we just had."

Keiko leaned back and captured his gaze.

"Oh? Then what else?" she asked.

"For taking the leap with me by being here when I got back. I promise that you won't regret taking this step, whatever it is, with me."

She kissed him and smiled.

"Music to my ears."

10

"I can't believe that I'm here. This place is amazing! Why haven't I come here to visit you before now?" Madison asked the moment she and Keiko arrived at Keiko's place on the island.

She laughed when Keiko looked from her to her luggage and then back to her again. She knew that look on her friend's face. They had traveled together before. The focus was on the luggage.

"I don't know but you have enough luggage to make me think you're not going back home. Are you sure you're only here for a few days?" Keiko laughed.

"I promise I am not here to invade your space for more than a few days. On the plane ride in, we passed by the suites that are built into the mountains. I've never seen anything more romantic than that. When I get a man, a good man, I'm going to make sure we come here to get it in. I notice that they are all glass enclosed but we couldn't see inside from the plane. I'm glad that the plane comes down far enough under the clouds to allow for that view. I assume that's the whole purpose of flying by them upon landing."

Keiko lugged all of Madison's luggage into the bedroom. She came right back out to answer all of Madison's questions. Before she could, Madison walked by her and into the bedroom. She followed her back in.

"Those units have one way glass. The guest can see out but any planes flying by with people on them can't see in unless the guest flips a switch to activate or deactivate a privacy screen on the glass enclosure. It's the perfect romantic getaway. That was all Byrum's idea. There are only ten of those units. The resort isn't even open to the public yet and those suites are already sold out for the first two years. There is a long waiting list for them. When they're ready for viewing, one day I'll take you so that you can see the inside of the mountain. That's the amazing part. The hotel and all of the amenities are built inside. Each room comes equipped with service that you never have to open the suite doors for. They are the best in peace and quiet without the need for do not disturb sign. That's a given."

"I can't wait. I'm already impressed by what I've been hearing and what I've seen so far. Are you sure you're good with me staying here? You have a lot of space, but still, I don't want to intrude. I told you that I can stay in the other bedroom. I know it will be Tru's room this summer. I don't want to put you out by staying in your room. I'm already thankful that I didn't have to pay for a hotel. Your place is nice. It's big. What is it, two bedrooms and two baths?"

"Yes. It's only mine while I'm here working. I'll have to give it up when I eventually move back to Detroit. I want you to stay in my room. You'll love the view of the ocean. I see it every day. I want you to take it in each day that you're here."

While Madison made herself comfortable lounging across the bed, Keiko pulled out extra towels and other toiletries, just in case.

"When is that?"

"When is what?" Keiko asked.

"When are you moving back to Detroit?"

"I don't know yet. There is still a whole lot to do. I'm only thinking about being in the here and now."

"Does that mean that things are going great with Byrum for you're here and now newfound attitude? Before you answer, just know that I love this new you."

Keiko forgot to take out the information on the resort to share with Madison. She raced to her nightstand to take it out and took the few seconds to smile her way through the time she and Byrum had been spending together for the past two weeks. They didn't chance her spending every night with him. She was happy that they were able to slip away to his apartment when they wanted downtime together. They couldn't do it at her apartment because there were too many eyes around with the staff all living onsite.

She was happier than she's ever been in her life. That was because she finally let go of any reservations she had about being with him. Deciding to just go with where life was taking them was working. She turned her attention back to Madison.

"He and I have found our rhythm. We're keeping things under the radar from others. When we're at the office, it's all business as usual. When we're together, I swear, I can't get enough of him."

Keiko started fanning herself. Like a true friend, Madison saw a magazine, picked it up and began to fan her friend as well. What's a good friend if you're not helpful. They both stopped moving when they heard a sound. Their eyes darted about here and there.

"Whoa, somewhere a phone is vibrating," Madison said as they moved about to find whose phone it was,

Keiko realized it was hers. DeConnor was calling.

"One sec. Hello?" Keiko answered.

"Hey. I was hoping we could talk a few minutes about Tru's visit. If he's still going to be with you, I need to know how long. If I don't need camp for the entire summer, I don't want to have to pay for it. They give up to three weeks a year for vacation without having to pay. I haven't used any so far."

"I think it depends on when he has to go back to school. I was hoping for at least six weeks. I can cover the cost of the additional time he won't be there that you're being charged. That's not a problem."

"Keiko, I can pay for my son's camp costs and before and after school costs, or whatever it's called now that he only goes full-time in the summer now that he's in school. You can keep your money."

The sting of his curt words would usually sting. Keiko was in a different place now. She brushed it off. She looked at the phone before putting it back up to her ear. Why DeConnor was being tense with her she didn't know. How every conversation with him starts this way, she didn't know. She held onto her patience and let his apparent attitude fly by her.

"You don't have to get testy about it. You brought up the cost and I was just trying to offer it since he'll be with me. I don't want to fight with you about this. When are you thinking of bringing him out here? Should I come and get him? I mentioned that when I was home."

"I'll still bring him to you. Listen, while I'm there, I was hoping we could talk about something."

For some reason, his voice softened. That gave her concern. These days, he was usually angrier with her than not. She responded cautiously.

"About what?" she asked.

"Us. I want to talk about us," DeConnor replied quickly.

Keiko already knew she wasn't interested but she didn't tell him that. There was no doubt that her mother and maybe her father too, had been talking to him like they have been talking to her. If that was the case, the conversation would be over before it started. The only things they needed to discuss going forward were those that had to do with their son. There was no *them* that she was open to discussing. She was done. Now wasn't the time to get into it with him; not with Madison in the room. As her bestie, they talked about a lot but she didn't want to talk with him in front of her.

"Did you send me the information on the date you plan to arrive? I'm off for a few days now because Madison is here for a visit. I want to put in for time off while Tru is here. We have a daycare and camp onsite here at the resort for employees with children. He'll be there when I'm working, though my work time will be limited when he's here. I've already cleared that with Byrum."

"Oh? How is your boss? I saw a story about those Blackstone brothers and how well their resorts and other business deals are going. He's swimming in money. What's his worth these days, about thirty million or so? That's per brother, I hear. Good for them. Maybe you can let me know if they are ever looking for investors. I may want to connect with them."

Keiko ignored him. This was a conversation she was not about to have with him. This wasn't the first time he brought up trying to connect him with Byrum or one of his brothers. Little did he know that none of them cared for him, nor would they discuss any business opportunities with him.

"Send me the date you're dropping him off. I'm planning a visit to my parents during the last few days he'll be with me. I can bring him home from Boston, if that works for you."

"Yeah, that works."

"Okay. Like I said, Madison is here and I have to go. I'll send you a text or email later this week about Tru's visit. Bye."

Keiko ended the call and tossed her phone onto the bed harder than she had planned.

"That was cold. Did he even get a chance to say goodbye to you before you hung up?" Madison asked, laughing.

Keiko chuckled too and smiled.

"He felt insulted when I offered to cover some of Tru's costs for camp. I know I shouldn't have been that cold or dismissive but I don't want him to think that he has to cover everything. I know he has the money to pay it with no problem. I wanted him to know that I have it too. He hates the idea of my independence."

"He always has wanted to keep you under thumb especially financially. He's one of those guys who thinks that he can buy anything and anyone with money. That's a bullet I'm glad you finally dodged. Better late than not at all."

Keiko couldn't agree more.

"Guess what? He asked about keeping him posted if Byrum and his brothers are ever open to having investors. He's interested, if so. The *nerve!* He has never even liked Byrum. He used to call him, *pretty boy*; and not in a flattering way. Now all of a sudden, he wants to possibly have a sit down about investing. DeConnor is crazy. He will be waiting a lifetime for that. Plus, he wants to talk about us. There is no us!" Keiko yelled, picked up her phone and threw it on the bed again; just because.

Madison stood and took her by the hand.

"Okay, I need you to calm down. You are not the Keiko that he led around on an invisible leash. You are your own woman. You don't have to hook him up with Byrum. You don't have to talk to him about you and him if you already know the answer is no. Say that and move on. He is controlling. That is not going to change. What has changed? *You*. Do you know what else has changed? You're in love. Live in that."

Keiko heard the words and knew them to be true.

"I can't believe I let myself fall in love with him. Not DeConnor, though that sentiment is a given. I'm talking about Byrum," she said, sitting on the edge of the bed next to where Madison finally sat back down.

She let her head hang down knowing that she was in a bind. She and Byrum were having fun. She wasn't supposed to fall in love.

"Honey, you did not just fall in love with Byrum overnight. That pot has been brewing for a long time. It's only now that you have finally allowed yourself to love again. You could not have picked a better man to fall in love with. The question is, how does he feel? Does Byrum know?"

Keiko shook her head vigorously from side to side.

"Of course not. I wouldn't dare. He has vowed to never fall in love again. Besides, what kind of relationship is this? We can't go out in public and do couple things. We can't take romantic trips together. We can't walk around holding hands and kissing anytime the mood strikes, no matter who is around. We have these beautiful, romantic cabanas on the beach. I love them so much. They are similar to the ones on *Secret Whisper*. You've been there. I can't spend a night there with the man I love because I'm not supposed to be in love with him. I remember Cheyenne telling me about the first night that she and Tellum spent the night in one. She said it was the most romantic experience of her life, at that point. Of course, Tellum has been wowing her with nothing but romance since then. I wish I could do things like that with Byrum. I wasn't supposed to fall in love. How can I tell him that he's the best thing that has happened to me outside of having my son without scaring him away? These stolen moments with Byrum are everything to me. I don't want them to end by revealing I've fallen in love with him. He would run for the hills. After what happened with his ex, I know the last thing he wants is hearing words of love from another woman; at least, not yet."

"Tell him the truth. I bet he's in love with you too. Did you think of that?"

"No. All I can think about is if I tell him and he rejects me, my world will crumble. I don't know how to live with that at this point. The way he treats me is new to me. It's never happened to me before. I feel like a cherished princess. He likes to give me full body massages. He cooks for me. We cook together. He tells me about things that bother him. I get to celebrate with him through kissing and sex when he wants to celebrate. He notices everything about me. He sends me sweet texts. He can't send me gifts at work but when we're together, he buys me sweet things like little shot glasses that I love collecting. You know I love those little souvenir bells. He was on a recent trip to Milan and came back with a bell from there. He's thoughtful like that. He knows what I like without me telling him everything I like and don't like. He pays attention. What's not to love? He's an incredible man."

"Talk to him. Don't think that being in love with him is a

bad thing. It's not. What you'll need to worry about is what will happen when the day comes that the two of you get so serious that you're ready to tell people. Do you know where the problem will come in? DeConnor."

Keiko knew that. From the start, going back to the night of the wedding when her trueness about Byrum came to the surface, she knew that DeConnor finding out would be a knife in her ex's chest.

"I know what you mean. I've thought about that too."

"No one else will care as much as he will. If it's his plan to get you back, then once you tell him that it's not happening and that you're dating Byrum, he will blow a gasket. Talk to Byrum about next steps. Tell him the truth about how you're feeling. Just not today. Today, we're going to remove all of this misery around us and buy some incense or something. I don't want anything bad on your mind while I'm here. I want all fun, fun, fun. Do you think you can control yourself for a few days without having to ride that *Babyface* of his?"

Keiko laughed and punched Madison playfully on the shoulder.

"I think I'll be okay. I know where to get it when I want and need a Byrum fix. I will admit that he has released a sex demon in me. We can go from slow, sexy, passionate love in the shower or in bed to wild, out of control, back-breaking sex on the kitchen counter. No limits on the sexcapades, that's for sure. I didn't realize I could be such a freak!" Keiko triumphed.

"See, you're already feeling better. Think good things about *Loverboy* and then tell me what we're doing tonight. I hope it's something fun and not just dinner and dancing. Y'all got stripper joints around here? I want to see some beefy men! I want to see and feel on some man-meat, and I mean that in the most literal sense of the word," Madison cheered.

"I'm sure you brought a hooker dress or two with you. Yeah, we're heading out to a strip club tonight. Don't forget – I'm your bestie. I know you better than you know you. I got us reservations because that joint be *packed*. I think I've seen the walls sweating. No reservation, no entry. First, let's get dinner at this spot off the resort that I think you're going to love. Before that, I want to take you on a tour around the resort. We can stop off at my office so that you can say hello to everyone. Some of them you know from back in Detroit. Others are new and live here on the island all the time."

"Is Byrum there today?"

Keiko rolled her eyes and smirked.

"You are relentless. Yes, he's in the office today."

"Good. I need to get my eyes on *Babyface* now that I know you're all in love and stuff."

"You can't tell him that you know. Stop calling him that. No harm, but every time you say it, I want to burst out laughing."

"Girl, am I your bestie or not? I wouldn't tell him what I know; never. I do want to be in the room one day when you tell DeConnor. I want to delight in his disappointment; in his jealousy. He thinks he loved you. He wouldn't know how to treat a woman if someone provided him with a step-by-step guide. He treated you like property. I'm just glad you finally walked away. You're happy now. You love a fantastic man. Most of all, that body of yours is experiencing real love and true lovemaking. Also, hot, untamed, feral, spicy, amorous sex. Get yours, girl! Let's get out of here. I want to see everything while I'm here. Feel free to throw one or two sexy men my way. When I get back home to my baby girl, I have to jump back into mommy mode. Oh, I'm also in auntie mode all the time too because my sister loves getting free babysitting while she runs the streets. Here, I'm unleashing all of me on someone! I am kid free. It's time for adult stuff!"

Keiko hopped up and raced after Madison as she left the bedroom. Grabbing her phone, it vibrated the minute she picked it up. It was a message from Byrum.

"Have fun with your friend. Don't worry about work. I miss you. I'm thinking about you, baby."

That made her smile from her heart. It was a heart that loved Byrum Blackstone with everything in her.

Keiko questioned if she could really be this gloriously happy.

"One day at a time, girl," she said to herself. "One day at a time," she repeated, adding an extra pep to her steps.

11

"Duron Knight! How the hell are you?" Byrum asked.

He and Duron had been playing phone tag for a few weeks. With five children under his belt, Byrum had to get in with Duron when he could.

"I can't call it. If I had your hand, I wouldn't need both of mine. How is life treating you?" Duron asked.

Byrum got up and closed his office door. His team was celebrating another birthday. He was planning to join them after his call. For now, he needed to drown out the background noise.

"I can't think of one complaint about my life. It's all good; it's actually great. You already know business is great. The family is well."

"That wedding of Tellum's was five-star stellar. Taija and I were talking about it last week."

"I'm happy that you were both able to attend. I know Tellum wasn't going to be happy if you didn't serve as one of his groomsmen."

"Man, it was good to get away. With five kids, it's not easy to do all the time. Taija doesn't like to leave the kids for too many nights without one of us being home. I was able to talk her into a quick trip back to *Secret Whisper* after the wedding in Detroit. When we got back home following the wedding and after checking all the kids to be sure they still had all their fingers and toes, we were good to go. We got on a plane and went to the island. One of the best trips of our marriage."

Byrum laughed along with Duron. He'd met him through Tellum. They were in the same fraternity, though different college chapters. Duron and his two best friends, Michael Bailey, who was now his brother-in-law and Tyrone Davis, own one of the fastest growing architecture firms in the country. Their firm and their magnificent team are the designers behind all of the development and upgrades at all of the resorts.

"How old are the kids now?" Byrum asked.

"The twins are about to be twelve. We also have a ten-year-old, a five-year-old and the baby is two later this month."

"You've been busy!" Byrum jested.

"My family believes in being fruitful and multiplying. It helps that Taija's mom lives with us. We also have a nanny who lives in our home most of the time. My parents are a great help as well. My sister and Michael are on their third kid and loving life in California. My brother Brian, who recently joined the family business and his wife Sherry just had their third child. Tyrone and his wife, Victoria are pregnant with baby number four. You know a reunion is crazy in my family, which of course includes Tyrone, though he's not a brother by blood."

"Wow. Family gatherings have to be a lot of fun. I bet it's a blast with the cousins all growing up together and close in age."

"You don't know the half of it, brother. What about on your end? Any of you have any little ones running around?"

"Not yet. Cheyenne and Tellum plan to have an entire

144

brood that I'm sure they are already working on. As for me, not on your life. The same is for Callum."

"Man, my guys and I used to be the same way. We assumed my sister would have a ton of them but me and Brian? Never."

"Loren was on a call with my team here a few weeks ago. She's under contract to design the interior of the new suites on the cliff as well as our dining halls and restaurants. She's already completed the work on the resort rooms. We'll do a video walkthrough with her when the team she is sending out does their final room check. She told Keiko that she was planning a visit soon to do her own walkthrough. She loves being hands-on and not just get information by way of the team she sends out to locations."

"It's such a pleasure working with you guys. She talks about working with you all the time. She and Michael were recently at *Secret Whisper*. She's already planning a return trip. I hear you're switching lawyers to Adrian Jarreau and his firm. You will find the best of care when it comes to your legal needs. Before we jump into work, I saw the stories about Valencia. I'm sure you've seen them too. How are you feeling about that?"

Byrum had been questioned by Tellum a few days ago about the situation. He'd informed his brother that Valencia had been calling him in Detroit and here at the island office. She was getting pissed that he wouldn't return her phone calls. He didn't have anything to say. If she was looking for a shoulder to cry on, he was fresh out. She lost that privilege when she made a fool of him.

"I don't feel any kind of way about it. That time in my life is over with. I'm sorry she's going through all of that. She made her bed. She made her choice. I get why she did it, but still, there is nothing there ever again. Besides, there is already someone else."

Byrum was about to go against every rule he had about his personal life with Keiko. He hadn't seen much of her since her best friend arrived on the island a few days ago. He did get to say hello on the first day. He was glad Keiko brought her by the office. That gave him a chance to see the woman who was on his mind day in and day out. He'd seen Madison before at various company events since Keiko first started working for them. He liked her.

"Anyone you want to tell me about?"

"If I do, it's your ears only, bro. Callum and my dad know. I haven't talked to Tellum about her yet. It's sort of sensitive."

"Okay, I hear you."

Byrum braced himself to share about his love for the woman who worked for him.

"I'm in love with Keiko Lee. Do you remember who that is?"

Byrum spun around in his office chair, unsure of his feelings about revealing what was going on.

"Remember? I spoke with her earlier today about this call. She called me to confirm that we were still on track for this discussion. What's the sensitive part? Is she involved with someone? Married? That doesn't seem like you, but hey, whatever floats for you."

"She's not either of those. You know who she is to me."

"Yes. I just heard you say you're in love with her."

"She's my executive assistant, D. It's tricky territory."

"Only if you make it. Do you remember how I met my wife? I was auctioned off at a bachelor sale for charity. She was the woman who purchased dinner with me. In other words, she bought me. Talk about an embarrassing event. If it had not been for that, I wouldn't have met the love of my life. You and your brothers know I live and breathe Taija and now her and my kids. You can't pick how, when or where you will meet the woman who makes you want to give up everything just to have her love. If that's you, I don't care what she does for work or that she works directly for you. If you love her, don't you dare let that go. Your history doesn't bode well for the woman who comes into your life after what happened with Valencia. If you're telling me you're in love with her, I know it's real. You have never pegged me as someone who arrives at that place in life haphazardly. I'm happy for you. If you need a groomsman one day, I still have my tux from Tellum's wedding!"

Duron was laughing so hard, Byrum had to wait a few seconds to get a word in.

"You got jokes. Don't pull that out just yet. I'm in love with her. We're enjoying each other in private. She wants to keep things quiet for now. I get it. I don't want her name becoming office storytelling as if we're having some kind of fling."

"Is she in love with you?"

Before he could answer, his office door opened and Keiko came in with her finger over her sexy lips to let him know that she knows he's on the phone. She had a folder that she placed in front of him and put her finger where he needed to sign on two pages. He halted his conversation while he did so. He handed her the folder and winked at her. She blew a kiss at him, winked and left his office. She was finally back in the office and hopefully was ready to make time for him now that Madison had left the day before. Her son was coming in two days. He knew they would only have tonight for some time until Tru returned home. He wanted to make tonight special.

"Yeah, I believe that she is. Neither one of us are saying so. Her past is just as rocky as mine. Nothing is going to come between us, though. I won't let it. When she's ready to tell the world, I'll be ready. I think the team we have is openminded enough to mind the business that pays them. They know better than to indulge in gossip. I'm always clear about that. Anyway, let's get to the issue at hand."

Byrum sat up straight in his chair and hit the keyboard on his desktop computer. When the screen lit up, he searched for the package that he and Duron were about to discuss. If nothing else, Byrum felt good that he was able to share his news about Keiko within another person. It's clear Duron understood. A *bachelor auction*? He chuckled to himself and focused on the meeting. Duron was a true example that you can never plan for how you meet the person you want to love forever.

**

After a long day of running around, it was late in the evening and Keiko wasn't going to leave until after Byrum's last meeting of the day. When she walked into his office, his back was to her where he stood looking out of the large window at some of the construction happening a few floors below them.

"Tired?" she asked, breaking into his thoughts.

That was clear when he turned around with no emotion on his face.

"Exhausted," he revealed.

"You have one more call with a Trinity Holmes out of Mexico."

"No more meetings. I just want to go home and relax, hopefully with you? Are you free for dinner at my place tonight? We can order in."

"You want to cancel the call at the last minute?"

"It's seven in the evening here but it's noon in Mexico. She'll be okay. I didn't cancel late in the evening. I've had back-to-back meetings or calls all day. I just want to relax. Plus, I've missed you."

Byrum spoke low enough that no one could hear him other than her. She moved closer to his desk when he sat down.

"I've missed you too. Tru is coming in two days. I don't know if we'll be able to spend any time together outside of the office."

Byrum understood. His love for her would carry him until they could be together again. Knowing they both would be looking forward to that was enough for him.

"Tru is the priority. That is one sacrifice I am always willing to make when it comes to us. Can I have tonight? Are you free?" Byrum asked again.

Keiko leaned over his desk to speak directly to him.

"I already have an overnight bag packed and ready to go. It's Friday. DeConnor is flying in with Tru on Sunday."

When Byrum beamed up at her, her heart melted and she fell even deeper in love, if that were possible.

"What time? Can you stay until Sunday?"

"Yes. The flight lands late in the afternoon that day, so I'm all yours until then. I have a taste for Chinese food, with some grilled lamb chops, brittle cheesecake and...you."

"Baby, you are always reading my mind. I'll meet you there."

"I'll call and cancel your call with Trinity."

She was set to leave when Byrum's words stopped her.

"I'm glad your son is coming. He will love it here. Does he swim?"

"He does. Like a fish," she said.

"Well, I don't have to be present, but if you want, you can use the pool at my building since kids are not allowed to take part in any amenities here at the resort, even before we're open. Camp does not include swimming since the pools aren't kid friendly. Our license and insurance don't cover kids on the premises in the pool."

She nodded her understanding. There is a lot that the daycare and camp do provide that she's appreciative of.

"Tru would love that. Thanks for offering. My kid will be an Olympic swimmer one day. He's like his momma – a fish when it comes to water."

"I like seeing you covered in water. My shower misses you."

"Well, I just may be in it when you get to your place tonight. I don't know. I'll keep the mystery in the air. I'm already thinking of how I can help you relax and unwind. Can you leave that up to me? I know you love taking the lead but this time, it's my turn."

"Whew, baby. Don't threaten me with a good time. I might fly out of here and beat you to my place."

"I like the sound of that. Whoever arrives first gets to be on top," she relayed.

Adding a swift lick of her lips got the rise and smile out of a tired Byrum that she wanted.

"In that case, I will happily hang back a few extra minutes to allow you to get there before me. Nothing beats the image of you on top giving me the ride of my life. Consider yourself the winner in every way."

"Are you sure? I don't know. The view from the bottom, even looking over my shoulder from all points is a pretty tempting level of encouragement for me to let you get there first."

Byrum laughed at her and placed his finger to his temple. She saw the wheels turning.

"You do have a point. I see what you see. I'll tell you what; we will share in being in the winner's circle. How is that for a compromise?" he asked.

"I'll see you there!"

Keiko sashayed out of his office and into her own. She made the call that she promised Byrum that she would make. She then gathered her things and made her way to her apartment. She had a man to see about love. Despite their sexy banter, she was planning to arrive first. Under or over him, any position was a good one when it came to Byrum.

12

Keiko was kicking herself for oversleeping at Byrum's apartment. Her plan was to be back at her apartment before DeConnor and Tru arrived. If island transportation from the airport was the same as it usually was, she hoped that they would be stuck in traffic which would give her a little more time to get to the resort. She checked the flight information after Byrum helped her hustle out of his place. He had even called for his car to take her back to the resort. She had initially declined so that she could avoid running into anyone that she would have to explain getting out of his car to. When she found out how long it would take a rideshare to get there as opposed to his private driver, she took what Byrum had to offer. After kissing him goodbye, she hopped in the car and they were off.

As they weaved through traffic, Keiko nervously bit her fingers, but not her nails. She relaxed back on the soft black leather seats and turned her mind to the weekend. That had her smiling from ear to ear.

It began when she beat him to his own apartment. She'd texted him that she had ordered dinner for them. She surprised him with a hot, soothing bath when he arrived. They got in it together. There were candles that provided a soft glow over the room, including the bedroom. She wanted a night of no television at all. She wanted them to be able to focus on each other. To reach that goal, she hid all of the remotes.

In that bath, sitting between his legs with her back to him, her head resting back on his chest, they talked about what was happening to them. Neither said anything about being in love, though love was in the air. Instead, they talked about sharing with close family and friends that they were involved. Revealing that they wanted to continue seeing each other but not keep it private any longer was their first step to love; she knew that and so did he.

First, they needed to talk to the team on Monday about them. They wanted to let those who worked closely with them each day to hear from them about how their newfound relationship came to be. They had discussed the risks and determined that what they were sharing was worth it. Going into a relationship with their eyes wide open was the only way they could see what the distance would be for them. That's all that mattered.

Her plan was to tell DeConnor while he was here. She was anticipating the conversation not going well, but it is what it is. She was telling him before they told anyone else in order to lessen the blow to him. The thought that he wanted to talk to her about them, probably getting back together, would thwart any chance of that happening. That was always the case for her.

It was DeConnor who was cockily thinking he could speak her back into his life and she would just go. Nothing could do that after what she'd been through. Not now, not ever. Still, she owed him the chance to know who would be in Tru's life. This way, she didn't have to hide away from Byrum the entire time Tru was here. She would spend each night at her own place, but perhaps, they could spend time with Byrum. She wanted Tru to get used to the man in her life being a part of their lives going forward. Tru knew Byrum as her boss but not as the man she loved.

The ride back to the resort seemed to take forever. The closer they got to it and she could see it, the more her legs trembled. All she wanted to do was beat DeConnor and Tru to her place. If he had arrived early, her team, the small group that worked on Sunday, would have had someone escort them to her apartment. That was the last thing she wanted.

Within minutes, they were pulling up. No doubt, Byrum's driver had ran a few lights and broken a few speed limits to get her here. Byrum was clear to the man that he was to get here back as soon as possible and safe. He did just that. When she offered him a tip, he let her know that Byrum had already taken care of it. Putting her money away, she got out and took her bag from the seat before running toward her apartment.

By the time she reached it, she was out of breath. There was no sign of DeConnor or Tru. She said a quiet thanks and prepared for their visit.

Not ten minutes later, there was a call to her cell to let her know that she had guests at the main entrance. She asked that they be escorted to her apartment. She couldn't wait to see Tru. Being away from him was torturous. She fought back tears. She was happy that he understood that the distance was only temporary. She made sure every moment with him counted whether it was in person or virtual.

Keiko paced nervously as she waited. She took the few minutes it would take for them to reach her to take one last look at Tru's room. Though no kids were officially allowed on the resort once it opened, they were allowed to have family stay with them as long as all of the rules for guests were adhered to.

She had gone out to the mall the week before and picked up all things Marvel, especially Thor related items and bedding. Tru loved his character the most. She had ordered a car shaped bed and added Marvel themed decals all around it. There were pictures on the wall, bedding, rugs and a small bookcase that she covered in stickers. She nodded her approval. It was a lot like his room at her apartment back in Detroit. She wanted Tru to feel like he was at home with her on the island.

The door buzzer rang and she raced to the door. When she opened it, seeing Tru's face light up as he leaped into her arms was all the greeting she needed. Their escort nodded to her and she nodded back, letting him know that he could go back to his duties. Her attention turned back to Tru. She couldn't count the number of kisses she had placed all over his face. When he started wiping them off, she knew he'd had enough.

"Mom!" he declared. The sound of his voice was a delight to her ears.

"I think you've grown in the few weeks since I last saw you."

"Oh, mom. You saw me on the screen."

She knew he was talking about the weekly, sometimes daily video chats they had.

"I know, but it's not the same as seeing you up close and everything. I know you're taller."

She then turned to DeConnor. When he tried to lean in for a hug, she grabbed Tru by the hand and walked further into her apartment. This was not the time for physical contact with him knowing they didn't do that anymore.

"Okay," she heard DeConnor say behind them as he closed the apartment door.

When he started to place Tru's luggage near the door, she pointed to the bedroom.

"Can you put those in his room. It's down the hall and to the right."

"Sure. Is this an overnight bag? Do you want me to carry this back?"

Keiko didn't know how to answer. She just remembered that she was in such a hurry when she got home that she dropped the bag she'd taken to Byrum's place in the floor and never picked it up. She should have known that DeConnor would pick up on it. He watched every move she made at all times. That was something she hated in their marriage. She couldn't breathe.

"No, you can leave that there."

"Are you going someplace or coming from someplace?"

"DeConnor? Tru's luggage, please?" she asked again.

"Right."

She didn't miss that he looked back at her bag again before he moved beyond it. She then turned her attention to Tru.

"So, tell mommy about your flight. It was long, wasn't it?"

"It was very long. I kept asking daddy how much longer. At first, he answered me then he stopped and told me to not ask him again because we would be here when the plane got here. I didn't like the food. I ate the sandwich daddy packed. He said he knew I wouldn't like the food. I did eat the chips and the pretzels. This is where you live?"

"Well, it is when I'm here on the island. Remember, I told you I work here. It won't be forever. I'll be coming home once this place is all built up. Mommy will take you on a tour in a little while. I have so many fun things planned for us to do."

Tru jumped up and down, not dropping the large red truck in his hands.

"Really? Can we go now and see? I saw a pool. Can I go swimming?"

"Not here on the resort but I have a friend who has a pool who will let you swim there anytime you want. He says it's okay."

"Is that friend, Byrum Blackstone?"

Keiko looked up to DeConnor standing behind the sofa where she and Tru had sat right in front of the television on the wall.

"What?" she turned her head and asked.

"Mommy, can I have an ice cream sundae? The kind with sprinkles and chocolate?"

She turned her focus back to Tru and away from the scowl on DeConnor's face.

"Yes. I think we can arrange that. The resort has the best ice cream sundaes. We'll get one with dinner. I'm thinking the Italian restaurant since you love spaghetti."

"Is that before or after his swim at your friend's place? I asked you a question. Are you talking about Byrum?" DeConnor harshly asked a second time.

Keiko was already losing her patience. She was ready for DeConnor to go back to the airport for his evening flight back home. It was hours away, but she didn't care. She wasn't up for his shenanigans today.

"What is it now? Why the Byrum kick all of a sudden?" she questioned.

Then she saw it. He had her phone, her personal phone in

his hands.

"He sent you a text. I could only see part of it but it looks like he's calling you baby and that he's missing you already. What the hell is that about?" DeConnor yelled.

"Do *not* curse in front of my son."

"Our son."

"When you're like this, I meant what I said; my son."

When Tru jumped with fright at his father's loud voice, Keiko pulled him close. She sat in horror that DeConnor had her phone in his hands.

"Why were you snooping in my room? I told you Tru's room was to the right. Mine is at the end of the call."

"Oh, so that's your answer to him calling you baby? You work for him."

"You shouldn't be in my room or going through my things."

"I didn't go through anything. It was sitting on your bed."

"You shouldn't have been in my room. We are not married anymore. You don't get free reign around here."

"You are the mother of my son. I have a right to know everything about your life."

Before she responded unlike she ever has before, Tru couldn't be present.

"Tru, baby, can you go into the room with all the Thor stuff in it and play? I left some puzzles and new books for you. I think there may be a new Thor figurine for you too."

"Yeah!" Tru hollered and ran down the hall.

When she saw that he'd found the room, Keiko stood and faced DeConnor head on.

"What are you, a play thing for Byrum Blackstone now? You know he has a reputation of bedding them and leaving them. Is that what you've become since you've been here?"

"What I have or have not been doing is none of your business. Since you want to dive into my personal life, yes, I'm sleeping with Byrum. We are in a relationship. As for what happens in the bed, it's more than I could have ever dreamed of considering what my experience has been. Trust me, you do not want to have this conversation. You don't want me to compare. It will not be a good look for you. Give me my phone?" she demanded, thrusting her hand out at him. When he didn't hand it over, she lost her cool. "Now!" she yelled.

She's never raised her voice to DeConnor before. She could tell the minute he was shocked that she did.

"Is this who you are now? You raise our voice to me? I'm your..."

She raised her hand to stop him.

"You aren't my anything. If you were about to say husband, I have papers that say otherwise."

"You're sleeping with your boss? Who are you?"

"I'm a woman in love with another man. I'm not just sleeping with him, though that is the most delicious part."

Keiko knew she was hitting below the bet but it felt good. She'd spent years being berated by him. All she had done was stand and take it. Not anymore. He held no claims to her other than being Tru's father.

"Were you sleeping with him when we were married?"

"What? You couldn't tell that I wasn't? Remember how you would force me to undress after a night out with my friends so that you could see if I had the scent of another man being on me or in me? That was the most degrading part of our marriage, especially when I wasn't the one stepping out. That was you, unless you forgot."

159

"When then? When did this thing with him start?"

"None of your business. I am no longer your business unless it comes to our son."

DeConnor walked from one end of the living room to the other.

"To think that I came here to talk to you today about seeing if we could repair what had been broken in our marriage. I was willing to go to counseling and everything. We were much better together than apart."

"For who? You? Don't kid yourself that there was any part of our marriage that was good for me other than our son. That is the only thing you gave me that I was pleased about. You were horrible to me. I would never go back to that. I am treated like a queen with Byrum. I took a lot from you in our marriage when I should have demanded better. You thought you owned me. I am free from you DeConnor; *free*. I love my life. I love Byrum. I was never going to consider going back to you."

"You think Byrum Blackstone, the womanizer, loves you? He doesn't know how to love any woman. He gets his jollies going from woman to woman."

"Oh, and you didn't do that behind my back the whole time we were married? Oh, I forgot – you paid for yours."

Keiko calmed because they were getting heated. She didn't want that. Hopefully, Tru couldn't hear them.

"You are so naïve."

"Am I? I was before. My eyes are wide open now. I trust him with me; with my heart."

"You know what, you deserve the heartache you'll get being involved with him. How come you haven't mentioned this to me before? I deserved to know, especially with Tru being here for a month. He'll be around my son, I'm assuming."

"He will see him, yes. He won't see any intimacy between me and Byrum because he's not ready to have that explained to him yet. He's five. He knows Byrum as a family friend and that's how it will be. I was going to tell you today. You happened to snoop in my room and picked up my phone after he must have sent that text. No matter what, you invaded my privacy whether you deserved to know or not. We decided last night that it was time to tell people."

"Oh, so no one knows? You've been letting him sneak you around? Like I said, you're a play thing. You should recognize and come out of the bubble you're living in. Good sex does not equate to love."

"Don't I know it. Bad, conforming and out of obligation sex doesn't equate to love either, but yet, I stayed."

"What, you're expert at sex now?"

"DeConnor, don't do this to yourself. You do not want to hear about my sex life. I know what I've been missing out on. I'm never going back. Deal with that. We are co-parenting and that's it. If you were planning on anything else with us, forget about that. Focus on Tru and that's it."

"I'm thinking that he should go back home with me. I don't think this is the time for him to be here with you and your rich boyfriend or whatever the hell he is to you. We have some things to talk about first when it comes to what he is exposed to in your life."

When DeConnor started to walk toward the bedroom, she walked ahead of him and stood her ground in front of him.

"You may have controlled me while we were married, but you don't anymore. I want to be very clear about something.

If you attempt to take my son back to the states right at this moment, he will get a front row seat to us wailing on each other because, no matter my stature, I will fight you to the death before I let you take my son away from me. Now, if you want to deal with this in court in the states, let's do that when I bring him home in a month. Until then, he's staying here with me. You can get on your plane back home tonight. Feel free to exit stage left out of my life. If you attempt to leave here with him, trust me when I say that everything in this apartment will become a weapon. Do not play with me when it comes to Tru."

Keiko remembered she had her keys in her hand. She gripped them tight, especially the container of mace on the end of it. When her hand moved to grip it tight, DeConnor looked down to her hand. When his eyes met hers, she knew what he saw; he saw a determined woman who would protect her son at all cost.

"Mace?"

"Don't try me. I'm not the squeamish woman you were once married to. You need to leave. You can see Tru in a month."

"Keiko."

"No! Just leave. I'm sorry you found out about me and Byrum like this. I was going to tell you. Now that you know, deal with it because your anger or jealousy won't change anything. I love him and I love my son. I'm having the life I want. It took me a long time to get here. Now that I am, I'm good. Again, for the last time, please leave."

With her heart pounding in her chest, she wondered what he would do. No time in their marriage has he ever struck her physically. His abuse was mental and emotional. She was immune to that the moment she received her divorce papers.

"This isn't over. Just remember this one thing – whatever comes next is because of this moment right here."

DeConnor looked down at her hand once more and then retreated. He went to the door and slammed it behind him when he left. She raced to lock the door. Then and only then did she actually breathe. Gathering herself, she plastered a smile on her face and went into Tru's room. Her son deserved to see her happy and living a good life. That was the mommy he was about to get for the next month.

13

"Mr. Blackstone, you have a visitor at the front desk at the main entrance to the resort," Sarai said over the phone intercom system.

Byrum looked down at his schedule and didn't see anything during this block of time.

"Who is it, Sarai?"

"He says his name is DeConnor Brooks. He's Keiko's ex-husband. Keiko isn't working today. She's not scheduled back for two days, on Wednesday. What would you like me to do? He's at the front gate. They haven't let him on the property. Security called and said not without your approval."

Byrum hadn't heard from Keiko since the morning the day before when he kissed her before she left to get in the car to head back to the resort to meet DeConnor and Tru. He was surprised the man was still here. According to Keiko, he was to return on an evening flight last night to Detroit. Perhaps, she'd had the talk with him about them and this was his showdown with the man. That or perhaps he wanted to talk business. Keiko mentioned he referenced if she could connect them on a business front.

"Go ahead and have him escorted here to my office. It's fine."

"Will do, sir."

Byrum grabbed his phone and dialed Keiko's number. He didn't want to interrupt her time with Tru, but he needed to know if DeConnor's visit was because of something they talked about. He would never back down because he was in love with Keiko. He had no problem sharing that with her ex-husband. He didn't care who knew. She didn't answer after three rings. He waited and was about to call her again when she called him.

"Hey, you," she happily declared.

"I guess you saw that I called."

"I did. I was actually on my way to the office so that the staff could meet Tru. Even the Detroit crew have never met him. I never brought him by the office when I worked there."

"Baby, listen. I only have a few minutes. DeConnor is here."

"He's where?"

"He's here at the resort. Security called from the entrance and said he was asking to speak to me."

"No. Don't do it, Byrum. He's angry."

"About? You told him."

"Not the way we planned. He snooped and saw the text you sent yesterday calling me baby and saying you missed me. We had a heated exchange."

"Are you alright? Why didn't you call me last night?"

"Because I know you would worry. I wanted to have a day of not thinking about him. My son is here and I wanted nothing but fun. By the time we got back to the resort last night, Tru and I both conked out and slept all night. We're just getting up and moving after his bath, which I didn't do last night. He was so tired. Did DeConnor say exactly what he wanted?"

"No, but I'll find out in a few minutes."

"You're letting him come to your office?"

"I am. He asked to see me."

"I guess he decided to stay another night. His flight was supposed to be for last night."

"You did mention that. Listen, it's all good. I'm a reasonable man. I also don't take mess off of anyone; you know that. We probably need to have this talk. Are you sure you're okay? I know how he has talked to you in the past."

"Oh, don't worry. It felt good to get my own word-licks in yesterday. After he left, I felt like sticking my chest out like Superwoman."

Byrum snickered.

"Superwoman, baby? That's news for you. I'll call you after he leaves."

"I'm on my way there."

"Maybe you shouldn't."

"Byrum, we're in this together, right?"

"Yes."

"I'll see you in a few minutes."

Byrum looked up right when the call ended to see DeConnor standing in his office doorway. He stood and walked around toward the door when it didn't appear that DeConnor was going to come inside. He looked beyond the man to Hank from the security team who had accompanied him across the resort to the office. Hank stood there, probably sensing that his visitor was up to no good.

"DeConnor. It's nice to see you again."

Byrum was lying but he needed to open the discussion for what it was going to be.

"No, it isn't. How long have you been sleeping with my

wife?"

So, the man was going to just jump right in with everyone listening. All eyes of the staff in the outer office space were on them.

"Okay, that's where we're starting. For starters, Keiko is no longer your wife. She hasn't been that for a while."

"How long have you been screwing her?" DeConnor shouted.

When Hank moved toward DeConnor, Byrum waved him off. He decided to let the man have the floor. If he found that DeConnor couldn't control himself, he had no problem body slamming the man to the ground in front of everyone. He kept a lighthearted disposition most times. When pressed, he could be a savage, especially with a man he knew had once treated Keiko in a disgusting manner.

"Since my brother's wedding. As you know, that was over a month ago, a long time after your marriage ended."

"She works for you. Shame on you, Byrum. Don't you care what that looks like? The appearance that gives? Of course, one of the mighty Blackstone brothers won't be impacted. It makes her look like a toy; a play thing. What is she, a placeholder until the next princess who decides to leave you for another man shows up in your life?"

Byrum leaned back against his desk, bracing his hands on either side of him. DeConnor was testing his patience. He thought about the dark gray suit, purple shirt and purple and lavender accented tie he had on and knew that he had no problem messing it up by dragging DeConnor across the hardwood floors. He held on to his patience.

"See, a less confident man would be insulted by that, but that's not who I am."

"DeConnor? What are you doing here?"

Byrum and everyone else looked to see Keiko coming up toward them.

"Where's my son?" DeConnor questioned loudly.

"I just asked my assistant, Sarai, to take him to the game room where he can play for now. He doesn't need to see or hear this. He got enough of an earful last night from what transpired between us shouting at each other. What are you doing here? You were supposed to fly back home last night."

"Not before I had the chance to speak to your lover. Oh, I meant your boss!" DeConnor stressed.

The look of horror on Keiko's face showed as she looked around at the staff who were all focused on her.

Byrum interrupted the silence.

"Enough, DeConnor. I would say let's take this behind closed doors, but at this point, I don't think it would matter. Let me be very clear about something. I don't care what you think you know about me and Keiko, but know this, I am in love with her. We are in a relationship. No one knew about it but us until now. I have no problem with this. I believe love is wherever you find it. I found it in her. I believe she found it in me."

Byrum looked to her to see her smile and nod her head.

"She told me yesterday that she was in love with you. How can this be? Is this what happens in the work setting? Secret relationships? Back group screws?"

That last word got Byrum up from his desk and walked up to DeConnor, bringing them almost nose to nose.

"You know what, Keiko confided in me about you. I won't put your business out in these streets, though you had no problem doing that with my and Keiko's business. Here it is. I will not tolerate your blatant disrespect of her at any juncture in life from this point going forward. I hope that you've released all negativity from your mouth that you needed to say. My security is here, but trust me, I won't need them. I love Keiko and she loves me. I have the kind of staff that knows that we are not offerings of office gossip. Keiko and I did not go into this lightly. We have talked and talked and then talked some more about the implications of revealing our relationship. We decided that what we have shouldn't be a secret. Now, thanks to you, it's not. We will go on loving each other. What you'll do at this point is up to you. What it should not include is disrespecting my lady in any way. Choose your words carefully before you continue on. If you're mad about it, that's on you. If you have issues with me being around Tru, I respect that as a man. You have every right to work that out with Keiko and I will step back; but only from that and not from her."

"Well, you can stand by her side when I take her to court for full custody. This is more drama than a five-year-old needs to be around. She's here living on this island, thousands of miles away from Detroit. She's sleeping with her boss. This isn't a good look for her. We'll see what a judge has to say. I came here to ask you to stay away from her, but you're right. She's not my wife anymore. She's yours now, I guess. I'll take my fight to the court system and we'll see who wins. By the time you get back to Detroit with Tru, I'll have you served. Thanks for letting me see what you're made of, Keiko. You're not the mother my son needs," DeConnor spat out, turning to face her.

Byrum was done with his presence.

"Hank, show Mr. Brooks to the gate. If he gives you any

trouble, feel free to drag him. Jalen, make sure he's never allowed here or at any of the Blackstone resorts."

"Yes, sir. On it."

As DeConnor walked by Keiko, he briefly stopped. Byrum raced over to be sure he didn't step out of line.

"I thought I wanted you back. Good luck trying to tame a playboy. I'll see you in court, Miss Lee."

The way he spat the words out, Byrum wanted to pick him up and slam him to the ground. That wasn't the kind of scene he wanted in his office. There had been enough entertainment already. Instead, he walked over and took Keiko by the hand. In front of everyone, including DeConnor, he kissed the back of her hand and then kissed her lips. When she kissed him back, placing a hand on his cheek and letting it rest there, he smiled against her supple lips. He would no longer hide his love from anyone. When the staff all cheered, he felt the tension in Keiko's body go away.

"He couldn't have you back anyway. He had better ask someone. We belong to each other," Byrum said before kissing her again, this time longer with added passion.

"We see you, boss! You got yourself a good woman," someone hollered.

"Yeah, and she got herself a good man," someone else said.

"They sure look good together," another voice hollered from the crowd just before cheering happened again.

"It's about time!" Sarai said walking to the crowd.

"Where's Tru?" Keiko asked her when she didn't see him with her.

"Kim at the daycare was there with other kids. They were playing games. She said she'd get Tru signed in so that he could eat breakfast with them. They were just about to be escorted to the daycare cafeteria. Is that okay?" Sarai asked.

"Oh, yes. That's perfect. He will love that."

"He was already having a good time when I stepped away. I wanted to see what was going on. I even brought Paul from the security team. I wasn't sure what was happening up here when you rushed in with a look of fear on your face and saying something about your ex being here to confront Mr. Blackstone," Sarai said.

Byrum let go of Keiko's hand as she walked over to Sarai.

"You said it's about time. You know?" Keiko asked her.

"I suspected. When I did, I was happy about it. The two of you are perfect for each other. That night when I saw you leaving the resort with your overnight bag and you gave me that story about checking out another resort, I suspected. Something about the way you were when you returned from the wedding clued me in. That and the fact that you were the only person here invited to the wedding. It's okay that you didn't say anything. I wouldn't have either. I'm happy for you."

"Really?" Keiko asked.

"Girl, hell, yes! I hope it's okay to say that. I am all about the love. Now, I do expect to hear more about this love thing at our next girl's night out. It will be your time to share some, but not all. We still have to work here," Sarai joked.

"Can I see you in my office for a minute, Keiko?" Byrum asked interrupting the chatter.

"Sure, you can. Keep it PG, kids. Also, keep the door open. These walls are not sound-proof," Sarai joked.

"Okay, everybody. The fun is over. Back to work," Keiko said before walking into Byrum's office and closing the door behind her.

Byrum wasted no time in pulling her close and finding the lips that he loved so much. Minutes later, he turned her loose.

"You love me?" he asked.

"You love me?" she countered.

"After what we've been sharing, I'm definitely taken with you. Most definitely in love with you. I'm glad everyone knows," he self-confessed.

Keiko walked away from him and sat down on the sofa along the office wall.

"He's going to try and take Tru away from me. He already has custody, though not through the court. When we divorced, I agreed to joint custody. What am I going to do now if he takes him away from me? That means even when I'm home, he will live full time with DeConnor if he wins. I have to go back home," she declared.

Byrum was surprised to hear her say she needed to leave.

"What? When?"

"Immediately. If he's going to start a war, I need to be ready. I need to reach out to my attorney. I can't let him win. I know the idea puts the office in a bind with me leaving. They can handle things. I can be patched in from Detroit. I can't let him go back and build a case without me knowing what's going on. I have to fight for my son. I want to stay and fight for me and you too. I'm torn."

Byrum sat on the large table in front of her and took her hands into his.

"Baby, I will be here when you're ready. I'm not going anywhere. I declared to everyone listening that I am in love with you. I don't take that lightly. I've fallen in love again because of who you are, not just who I am. I have nothing but time. If you need to leave, don't do it today. It will be hard to get a flight out. I'll have my plane checked and ready to take you back in the morning."

Keiko started to cry. He wiped her tears with the back of his hand.

"You don't have to do that. I know I've caused all of this drama. I'm sorry for bringing this to the office. I didn't mean for any of this to happen."

"You couldn't have predicted that he would be reading your phone. Baby, I'm in this with you."

"No, Byrum. I can't drag you into this. Keep your distance. DeConnor can play dirty; I mean *really* dirty. I don't want anything about us coming into the midst of this. I can handle him. I can't promise when I'll come back, but I will."

"I'll come to you. We should be able to at least do that. I don't want to be selfish. I know this is about your son and not me or even you. I need to exhale and pull myself back so that you can deal with this. I want you to know that if you need me, I am here; I'm right here. When I'm in Detroit next week, I hope I can see you. Let's play it by ear with whatever you think will work."

"Are you going to tell your family about us?" she asked.

"Callum and my dad know. I'm going to call Tellum in a bit before a call I have with him and a few other business partners. I'll call my mother later tonight. I love you, Keiko. As you leave here tomorrow, please take that with you. We both love again because what we have is real. Don't give up on that. I know it happened fast, but it did happen. I will never see that as something bad. Even if DeConnor tries to play it that way, we know what we feel. There is nothing wrong with that. Whatever you decide to do, whatever the fight is, when and where you need me, all you have to do is call me and I'll be right there. I'm in this with you."

She kissed him tenderly. There was something odd in the kiss, but he let it go. Instead of it feeling like they would continue at a later date, it felt more like she was saying goodbye. He didn't bring it up.

When Keiko stood to leave, he decided to walk her out. Maybe this would be the last time for a very long time that he would see her on the island again. They had kept the embers of their love flaming non-stop since they returned after the wedding. He wouldn't believe that she would let DeConnor's threat take her away from him. There is room in love and life for them to be in each other's lives. He guessed time would tell.

14

"Three weeks, Madison. It's been three weeks since I've seen Byrum. What if he's given up on us? What if he gets tired of me being in this fight with DeConnor? I can't believe he filed for full custody of Tru."

Madison came back into the living room of her condo after going in to check on their kids who were both napping.

After her morning spent with her attorney while Madison kept Tru for the day, Keiko was mentally and physically drained.

"Well, he said that he would and he did. The fact that he is making the love between you and Byrum look trashy is scary. He will demand that you tell every detail of your relationship with Byrum in court for everyone involved to hear. I know it will take a while, but the fact that a court could agree to re-visit your custody agreement behooves me. How can that be? You're not a bad mother. Divorced couples figure things out on their own when they have joint custody."

"I know. My meeting with my lawyer didn't go as planned today. Besides the fact that I'm missing Byrum like crazy, I feel trapped not being able to get on with my life outside of Detroit. I should be on the island finishing the work I started with that team. I never give up on what I started. I feel like I've let my team down by not being there with them. We all agreed to make the sacrifice to move there in order to help get the resort up and running."

"You're still working with them. You're able to go back to your work at the company here in Detroit. You connect with that team every day. You're still involved."

"I know, that's true. It's not the same. I was in a leadership position. My personal life invaded that and turned my world upside down."

"Did your lawyer say what you should do in order to fight this?"

"Are we ordering a late lunch? I know you don't feel like cooking and neither do I. I also don't feel like going home just yet."

"Let's order pizza and wings. The kids will be up in a few hours. Your lawyer?" Madison asked again.

"Yes. She recommended that I forget about going back to the island. She thinks that I am in a better position to keep the current custody agreement if I was here with Tru more often. When we signed the original divorce papers, it was that we would share custody. What ended up happening was that the opportunity for me to join the team on the island came up and DeConnor didn't have an issue. We agreed to work it out through communication. He loves his son. I don't question that. At this point, it's about him being jealous that I moved on. I should be allowed to move on without his approval. He's always been jealous of the Blackstone's and all that they have achieved. To find that I'm in love with Byrum sent him over the edge. He came right back after his encounter with first me and then with Byrum, and had his lawyer file for full custody. He knew that would break me."

"But it hasn't broken you. You're just going through. You

will come out on the other end with victory. No one can deny how much you love Tru and have his interest in mind with every move you make, including your love life with Byrum. I hate that you're going through this. Have you and DeConnor talked at all?"

Keiko rose from the sofa and went to the drawer where Madison kept menus for local restaurants.

"We'll order through DoorDash, but I want to see what I have a taste for before I pull it up on my phone in the app. He and I talked. He told me that I need to stay here in Detroit and consider our marriage again. If I agree to go to counseling and it doesn't work, then he'll drop everything and not fight me on anything. Can you believe that clown? I'm so sick of him trying to control my every move. This is all about me being with Byrum. I don't know if he would be this way with anyone else that I may have gotten involved with. He hates that it's Byrum."

"What's Byrum saying?"

"I talk to him every day. I miss seeing him and being held by him. He's got a business trip coming up. I think he's going to connect with Callum who is going through something. His brother broke up with that WNBA basketball player he was seeing. It's a whole big mess. I don't know the details. Byrum didn't know yet. He said he was extending a trip to meet Callum in Chicago. A friend of Duron's recently opened a new casino there. Callum was there with some woman or something and his girlfriend showed up to surprise him after seeing a post on social media that he was there. Whatever happened, it was enough to have her give Callum the boot. Byrum says he's drowning in his sorrow. Tellum and Cheyenne are in Florida at a wedding, so Byrum agreed to go and clean Callum up and get him back to Detroit or Hawaii where the other resort is being developed. Byrum and I talked about us. He says that there is still an us. I don't know. With these weeks between us, I feel a divide. I'm used to being around when he has down time. He has it without me around. That gorgeous hunk of a man could be with any woman he chooses. He chose me."

"No, girlfriend. He still *chooses* you. Don't speak about what you have in past tense. It's still fresh and alive. You're just feeling out of sorts because of the position DeConnor wants to put you in. You said he wanted you back. It's a crazy way to go about it, but that's what he's doing. First of all, he got you back here in Detroit full-time. Then he files for full custody in court. Next, he tries some plan about counseling and fixing a marriage that can't be fixed. It's not only broken, but it's been smashed into a million pieces and scattered all over the ocean. In other words, it's done. He hasn't realized that because he's DeConnor. It's how he thinks. He thinks with you being here, he's keeping you from Byrum."

"He is. I haven't seen him since I left the island. He was here recently but I had Tru for those four days. DeConnor is going back to the original custody agreement. I hope I'll get to see Byrum soon. I text him when my ex would have Tru again. Maybe, Byrum can fly in at that time. I would love even one night with him. Not to actually do anything sexual, though I'm craving that like a mad woman. I just want to be in his arms. I feel safe. I feel loved. I feel cherished when I'm with him. I miss that. I miss him."

"The kind of love that you and Byrum developed isn't going away simply because you haven't seen each other for a few weeks."

"Wait, did I tell you about Byrum's ex? These exes are coming out of the cracks in the sidewalk."

"Uh, oh. Do I want to know?"

"She finally reached him at the office. Sarai didn't know to not put her through to him. He said, like DeConnor is doing with me, she wants him back. Now that she's left her cheating husband and her father sees the error of his ways, he gave her his blessing to reconnect with Byrum. He says it's because he's rich now. He was on his way then, but now, he sees Byrum's potential. He sees the family as a possible ally in the business world."

"What did Byrum say?"

"He told her to get lost. He told her about me and she couldn't believe it. She tried to compare herself to me as if that would sway him. What the hell is wrong with people when someone turns them down. He said he wasn't interested and she resorts to trying to insult me. That only made him realize how much he loves me. Still, I don't know how long he's going to wait until all this drama with DeConnor is done. What if he gets tired of waiting?"

"He won't."

"He might," Keiko quickly responded.

"That man loves you. I know it's not a lengthy relationship, but it's love. That's all that matters for both of you. When do you take Tru back to his father?"

"Tomorrow. DeConnor will pick him up after school tomorrow. I will pick him up on Wednesday instead of after school on Friday. DeConnor has a business trip this week. I told him I would keep him all week, but he wants to see Tru before he leaves."

"You'll get a few days to figure things out. Why don't you

take a few days off and relax at your place. You've been on skates since you returned from the island. You need to regroup. Forget about DeConnor. Think only about Byrum. I don't care if it's phone or video sex, stay connected to your man. Not because you think he might get with someone else, but because intimacy, connection and relationship doesn't have to only be physical. Do it because it's a part of being in a relationship with someone."

Keiko pulled her phone from her back pocket where it was vibrating.

"It's Byrum. I'll take this in the bedroom. Order some food. Anything is good for me. Make sure there is chicken. Also, if you don't' have wine, order some from somewhere."

"Oh, bestie. You know there is always wine here. Still, there is room for more in my cabinet. I'll get some."

"I won't need a lot. A little will be good for me. I don't know about you, though," she laughed.

Keiko didn't wait for Madison to respond. She raced to the bedroom and answered the phone on her way.

"Hi, baby," she heard Byrum exclaim on the other end.

"Hi. It feels good to hear your voice," she said, laying across Madison's bed.

She had stopped quickly to check on the kids in the bunk beds in the room across the hall before she closed the bedroom door for some privacy.

"I want to see you. Being on the island isn't the same without you. Everyone is saying that. The team misses you. They don't miss you like I do, but we all have that in common. You play a big role on the team and not just in the role you play fixing my work life every day. You still do that, but from Detroit.

"I want to see you too. I'm mad that you were home recently and I couldn't see you. Thanks for understanding."

"Sweetheart, I told you that the priority is your son. We will make it work. There will come a time that our schedules will match. In fact, I'm heading to *Quiet Whisper* with Callum. I should be in Detroit tomorrow morning. I know it's late notice, but are you free?"

"Yes!" Keiko yelled and then pulled her excitement back. She didn't want to wake the kids.

"DeConnor will pick him up from school tomorrow. I'm free until Wednesday evening. I'm off tomorrow for a day I already had off. I have to work Tuesday and Wednesday before picking Tru up on Wednesday. Does that work? Before you answer, how is Callum?"

"In the jet sleeping it off. He was pretty drunk, but one of Duron's friends, Horace Grant, who co-owns that new Chicago casino helped me get him on the plane. He is out of it. I can't remember the last time I saw my brother this intoxicated."

"I'm sorry to hear he's going through something. So, is it what you thought?"

"Yup, Callum got caught with his pants down, literally. He embarrassed his girlfriend in front of her teammates. He was screwing one of his exes. He's done in Kendra's eyes. That's the woman he claimed he was really falling hard for but I guess falling inside of another woman was more important than what he was building with Kendra. That's sad because everyone likes her. She's done with him. Casted him out as if he was Thor like his father did him in the first movie. I used that reference because I know Tru has made you watch that movie a million times," he kidded.

"I actually understand your reference, so thank you for using that with something I could easily process. My mind is all over the place these days. You're taking him to Hawaii?"

"Yes, he needs a break. My cousins are there and will look after him. I'm going to have the plane turn around and bring me to Detroit. I'll be at my place. Do you want to come there or I can come to your place. What is easier for you?"

"I'll come to yours. I'm so sick of the four walls at mine. I could use the break."

"Okay, well, you already have the key and code there. Make yourself at home. I keep telling you that anytime you need a break, disappear from the world by going to my place. It's as much yours as it is mine."

"I know. I was there last week, just for one night. Everything smelled like you. I felt close to you."

"Well, you won't have to do that when I get there tomorrow. I should get in around eleven in the morning. You know we can work this out, right? Even if you stay in Detroit, that is still home for me. DeConnor can't control your life. If it helps that you're in Detroit, then you stay in Detroit. Just like Tellum did and does with *Secret Whisper*, I can go to the island when I need to. I have a very capable leadership team there. We can go together sometimes without you actually living at the resort and working out of that office. We can have a life together. I don't want you to think that anything has changed for me. I still want you as much as I always have."

"Me, too, Byrum. I love you. I only want you. I'll show you tomorrow. I'm way overdue."

Keiko moved around happily on the bed, turning over to the left and then to the right.

"Baby, you are speaking my language. Just don't give up

on us. Both of us have spent enough time with the wrong people to know that we've found the right one. Our desire for the greatest love of all brought us together. Nothing at all will make us question our love. Are you with me?" he asked.

Keiko wanted to cry. She'd been doing enough of that over the past several weeks that her life hasn't been able to be hers. She was going to fight DeConnor and anyone else who thinks that they can control any part of her life. Her life with Byrum wasn't just about being on the island; it was about being with him.

"I'm with you, always."

"Our love flourished on the island; it doesn't just live there. It's wherever we are. When this court stuff is over, we're going to talk about the next step in our relationship. For now, when you fight, I fight too. We're not going to let DeConnor steal our joy. We good?"

Keiko hopped up off of the bed and started boxing the air with one arm as she danced around the room like Muhammad Ali. She could hear Byrum laughing on the other end when he heard her grunts.

"We are perfect."

"What are you doing? You sound out of breath?"

"I'm up and started boxing the air. I'm planning to take this fight to the mattresses."

"We watch too many movies," he kidded. "No more Godfather or You've Got Mail movies for you," he kidded. "I'll see you tomorrow?"

"Yes, you will."

When the call ended, Keiko hurried back to the living room and plopped down on the sofa across from Madison. She knew all of her teeth were showing when she smiled at her best friend.

"I take it Byrum just made it all better? Did you have phone sex? If so, it had to be the quiet kind because I didn't hear anything," Madison jested.

"You're silly. No, we didn't have phone sex. He'll be here tomorrow. I'm going to have actual sex and lots of it."

"See? I told you. Trust that man and your love for him. It will all work out. Food is on its way. So are a few bottles of wine. Let's talk about this fight with DeConnor. What do you need from me?"

"Just keep being my friend."

"Girl, you've got friends galore here in Detroit just like you have on the island. I say we get the girls together for a night in with more wine, more food, dancing and girl chat. It's been a long time since the ladies have all been together. We need the girl group to get together to bad-mouth about DeConnor and his clown ass. I hate him so much. Wait, who sings that song, I Hate You So Much?"

Keiko got up and danced around the room while singing the lyrics.

"Girl, that's Kelis."

"Good. I'm going to download that from my Apple Music account right now. We're going to blast that when we get together. We'll even put up pictures of DeConnor to throw darts at and really make it a party! What do you say?" Madison asked.

Keiko didn't stop dancing when she gave her friend the thumbs up that she was all in. She could definitely use a girl's night out with friends. Madison was right. Life had gotten so busy for everyone that they forgot how good of a time they had when they came together. That reminded her that it was time for another girl's trip once things were settled with DeConnor. The last one they took had been unforgettable. That had been a week after her divorce had been final. They took a much-needed trip to Tulum to let their hair down.

"I'm ready for that."

"Do you know what else we should be ready for?" Madison asked.

"What?"

Keiko asked and stopped dancing so that she could hear.

"A girl's trip. This time let's go back to Secret Whisper and book one of those multi-guest bungalows."

Keiko's eyes widened with delight.

"Girl's trip!" she yelled. "We are so much alike. I was just thinking about the one we took after my divorce."

"All debauchery will be on the menu!" Madison added.

"Let's call the girls to discuss it. I have a big appetite. Let's discuss it over pizza and hot wings."

15

Byrum knew that he had to look rugged after spending more time in the air than on the ground over the past week. After finally touching down in Detroit, following changing his plans for heading to the *Silent Whisper* after his stop in Hawaii, he couldn't wait to get home to get some sleep. Most of all, he was overdue for quality time with Keiko. He was so used to being at the resort with her and connecting, that working in time with her on a personal level was an even bigger priority after all that had taken place just when their love was about to flourish. Just as they were about to be free to see each other without secrecy, the world collapsed around them. With Keiko back in the states and preparing for a court battle, he feared that the newness of what they were to each other may not survive the fight and the distance. If they could have found the time to be further along in their relationship, he may feel more like they were on solid ground. Still, it was his task to stay on the island to keep the opening of the resort on track. Coming to see Keiko before returning to the island was as much for her as it was for him. Too much was going on that could put their love at risk.

Most disturbing was his call with Valencia, whom he hadn't talked with since that last conversation about her marrying someone else. For her to reach out to him to try and get back in his life as if she hadn't blown it up a year ago mystified him. Being a princess really has done a job on her ego.

Since turning her down on all fronts, she hasn't stopped reaching out to him. Thankfully, he wasn't at *Silent Whisper* where she called and got through to him. He has since alerted his team to not put any calls from her through to him. He had no plans of entertaining anything she had to say.

As his driver made his way through traffic to get him to Keiko, he remembered that he'd promised his mother that he would check in with her to give the latest update on Callum. When he had taken his brother to the one place he knew he would get some distance from his own personal drama, he waited a few hours to be sure he was good before he left him in the capable hands of family they had who lived there.

Callum was a wreck by the time he got him to Hawaii, his second home. He took out his phone and called his mother, hoping she was available to talk. Once he got home to Keiko, he was planning to turn all electronic devices off for as long as she was with him. While on the plane, he'd met with teams at the resort and they all knew what to do in his absence. For that, he was grateful about the choices they made when it came to team leadership. They didn't just bring in people for the sake of calling them leaders who like to be in charge. They hired people with true leadership ability.

"Byrum, I've been waiting to hear from you," his mother said after answering on the first ring.

"I know and I'm sorry, Mom. My life has been all kinds of crazy lately."

"How is Callum? Is he devastated about the breakup? I tell you, you and your brothers and your back and forth with women. What was he thinking?" she asked.

"That, I don't know. What I can tell you, and Callum can go into better detail, is that she was hoping to surprise him in Chicago after seeing a social media post. I have told him about letting people either photo or record him when he's out and about. Boy, was he surprised. I won't tell you what she walked in on, so let's not have that discussion. This isn't the first time Callum has been this messy. It is the first time that he's been in a committed relationship where it seems, he wasn't as committed as he claimed to be."

"Kendra caught him with that Tessa girl, right? I never liked Tessa. I really like Kendra. She's a woman with her own lane in life. She didn't look to Callum to define her. I'll call him later or sometime tomorrow. I'm so mad at him. Had he sobered up by the time you got him to Hawaii?"

"Oh no. Too much alcohol in him by the time I got to Chicago. I had him checked out by a doctor before we flew to Hawaii and once we got there as well. He was good. He just needs to sleep it off. He slept the entire plane ride, which is odd for him. I had work to do, so I let him sleep, though I kept nudging him to be sure he was still with me. He will have one hell of a headache, for sure. He was still pretty groggy. Chief and Lola met me at the airport."

They were Blackstones who lived on Hawaii; born and raised there.

"He had better be lucky he has people who care about him. I'm going to miss Kendra. She doesn't seem like the type who would give him a second chance."

"At this point, I think if she did, it would be more like a fourth or fifth chance."

Byrum wouldn't share Callum's past with women. He was

the worse of the three of them when it came to the number of notches on his bedpost. Still, he had sympathy for him. Callum would never admit it, but he was in love with Kendra. Messing around on her showed his insecurity around commitment. Byrum knew he wasn't one to talk. He'd had his share also. He knew Callum would overcome this time and get back to his old self.

"I can't with him. How are you? I need you to slow down some. I will say, we haven't talked a lot since you told your father and I that you and Keiko are an item. Can I do my happy dance now or wait until we're off the phone?"

Byrum smiled knowing that his mother had put a relationship between him and Keiko out in the atmosphere way before they had hooked up after the wedding. His father told him all about it.

"Dance whenever you want. I'm pretty happy about it. In fact, I'm heading to my place to see her right now. After she dropped her son of at school this morning, she went there. I think she's a little under the weather. She sounded kind of out of it earlier this morning. She was going to drink some tea and lay down."

"Do you need me to make her my homemade chicken noodle soup?"

Byrum should have known that was coming the minute he said Keiko wasn't feeling well.

"Let me check on her first. I can always have some soup delivered if she wants it."

"You will do no such thing. My soup healed all three of you whenever you were sick. I'll check on her later. What do you say to bringing her to dinner at the house soon? I would love a chance to get to know her and have her know us. Is it too soon for that? I take it that you're very serious about her or you wouldn't have told us. You only tell me about women you're interested in for more than, well, you know how you boys are."

What she hinted at had him putting his phone on mute to laugh out loud. Having three sons who loved all things soft and female couldn't have been easy for her in their house. He took the mute off. Thankfully, their father shielded her from there ruthless behavior as boys growing up and finding out about all things sex.

"Mom, there has only ever been one other woman besides Keiko. Those others were just...let me be safe and say, friends. I don't think it's too soon. I'm in love with her. I think dinner would be great."

There was a long pause. For a minute, he thought that the line had disconnected.

"I'm happy to hear that. I know how hurt you were. I didn't want that to mar your take on love, relationship and marriage; not that I'm saying you're at a marrying stage with Keiko. I had hopes of someone. I want to see all three of you happily married and of course, with children. What does a mother have to do to get her sons to get married and give me some grandbabies? That is every mother's dream, eventually."

"Look to Tellum and Cheyenne for that. I can talk to Keiko about the dinner. Let me know if you have a date in mind. We work around her schedule with her son. Her ex-husband has issues with me. Because of that, we connect when her son is with his father."

"We can work around that. How is Keiko handling things?"

"It's rough on her. She may not be able to come back to

work at the resort like she has been. She's back to working in the office here. She still loves that, but her heart is with the new resort. This resort is the baby of my team and she plays a big role in seeing it come to fruition. She's still running things from here, thanks to technology."

"I knew she was perfect for you. I don't know much about her, but there was something about her aura. You know how I am about that. I'm glad she's more than just, what you call, a friend."

"You're right about that. I just wish that I could help her more with what she's going through."

"Be there, Byrum. That's what she needs more than anything. She needs to know that you're there. Back when your father and I dated, I went through some family issues. I can say that him being there when I needed him was more important than anything to me. He loved showering me with gifts and we took trips and things, but being that ear, that shoulder, getting a hug or just sitting with me and holding me was all I needed. Only help where she asks you to. I know how you are. You are the son who leads with his heart. You want to help everyone. Don't overstep, especially when it comes to her ex-husband. I'm not sure how you handled things when he visited you, but I wasn't there. I'm just happy things didn't come to blows. You're also a hothead. Take Keiko's lead. I'll check with Cheyenne and Tellum about dinner. It would be great to have everyone there. Callum, for sure will be there, whatever the date is. Even if I have to drag him away from Hawaii by his ear."

"Oh, I know you will. I've been dragged by you a few times. It's not pretty. In fact, it's quite painful. I'm sure he will comply. Thanks for being open to Keiko."

"Oh, please. I knew she was for you before you did. Of course, I'm open to meeting and getting to know her. If she means a lot to you, she means a lot to me already too."

"Thanks for always being there for us, especially me. I'm going to call you later. I just pulled up to my condo."

"I'll send you a text about dinner. I'm thinking my pot roast and potatoes with onions, carrots and celery, my baked macaroni and cheese, some fresh collard greens, barbecue chicken, chef salad and some kind of pie, for dinner."

"Apple cobbler."

"Okay, because you requested it first, that's what I'll make. Tellum will fight for peach cobbler. I'll make him a small one to take home. I love you, son."

"Love you too, Mom."

When he exited the car and walked into the lobby of his building, he waved to the attendants at the main desk when one of them pointed beyond him. When he turned his head, the two people standing and waiting for him didn't give him a good feeling. He started to walk away, but figured, now is as good a time as any for a chat. He left his luggage at the main desk where the attendant placed it out of sight and headed in their direction.

"Byrum."

"What are you doing here?" he asked of Valencia and her father aggressively.

"Son..."

Byrum turned his attention away from Valencia to her father, Prince Gastaud. He still wondered how he could be a prince and his daughter can be a princess. He thought that title would be reserved for her mother. Either way, he didn't care. He didn't like coming home to find them in the lobby of his building. He knew they kept a place here, which is how he had first heard about the new construction when he bought his condo. He assumed that after everything had gone down and her father wasn't in Detroit as much as he had been, that the man had either sold or rented his place on the second floor. He hadn't seen either of them in a year. That wasn't saying much. He doesn't spend a lot of time here himself.

"Don't call me son," he replied with a more abrasive tone than he had planned.

He father raised his hands, palms up as if he was surrendering.

"Look, I was hoping to talk to you," he said.

"How did you know I was in town?"

Byrum didn't believe in coincidences.

"I have a friend whose son works for the airport. I asked him to let me know the next time he saw your jet with you on it. The last few times, I wasn't in town. I'm here on business and I got a call that you'd flown in," Valencia admitted.

"What the hell? Why are you minding my business? We have nothing to talk about. That goes for your father as well."

"Byrum, I know you don't want to talk to me or see me. I don't think trying to have a phone conversation is a good idea when what I want to do is apologize to you in person. I know the move I made was a dirty one," she explained.

He was about to reply but her father spoke first.

"That's completely my fault. She hasn't been happy since I made her marry someone she didn't love. As I'm sure you know, that didn't turn out well. Trying to make my daughter live by old ways wasn't my best day. I was in a corner in the business world. I know it's crazy to think that there are ways like that still around when it comes to arranged marriages. I'm working to do away with that. I was hoping I could talk to you. If you would just hear me out, I would like to explain."

Byrum started to walk off and stopped.

"There is no need to explain anything. I've moved on in my life. Valencia should do the same thing."

"She really loved you and I ignored her pleas. Listen, can you give me a few minutes at the deli next door. Fifteen minutes of your time is all I'm asking. It's more about business than personal, but there is some of both. That's why Valencia is here with me. We were already here in town and I would hate to leave with bad blood still in the air. I promise, just a few minutes. If you never want to hear from us again, my daughter and I will respect that."

Byrum looked to the elevator and back to them. If these fifteen minutes would get them to leave him alone, he would do it. He hated loose ends. Truth is, what was left between him and Valencia was still unknown. They never did have any kind of closure. As for business, he couldn't wait to tell her father he wasn't interested. If he didn't do it now, it may come up again. That's something he didn't want.

"You have fifteen minutes and that's it."

Byrum walked out ahead of them and marched next door to the deli. He sat, crossed his legs and folded his hands on top of his knee. He looked at the clock on the wall and noted fifteen minutes for when he would stand to make his exit.

**

Madison didn't know what was ailing Keiko. It could be nerves, perhaps a pregnancy, but god forbid if it's a nasty cold, flu or pneumonia. The way those are taking people out of here was scary.

When she and Keiko had spoken earlier, she offered to

bring her something to soothe her upset stomach. She offered to stop by Byrum's place to bring her a few things, especially some soup and much better tea than those flimsy bags she kept in a zip lock bag in her purse.

When her taxi pulled up to the front entrance to Byrum's building, she was about to get out when her eye caught a glimpse of him sitting at a table in the deli next door. What she didn't expect was to see Byrum's ex-girlfriend and some man sitting at a table with him. They looked too cozy for her. Her blood really boiled when she saw Valencia reach across the table and place her hand on top of Byrum's as she talked. She didn't care what the conversation was about, they shouldn't be there at all.

She didn't want to be seen by Byrum. She had to get out of the car. Keiko would already be either in the lobby or on her way down to the lobby to get the bag of soup, crackers and some other items that she'd picked up from the store while on her way to work for her shift that would start at two.

After asking the driver to pull up a little further, she hopped out and saw Keiko walk up to the glass door where she waved at her.

"Hey, girl!" Keiko said the moment she walked into the building.

"Um, hey. How are you feeling?"

"A little better. I think I have some kind of bug or something."

"Well, this soup will fix you right up. So, Byrum?" she asked Keiko. She only said his name to start the conversation.

Madison didn't want to cause an issue, but Keiko was her best friend. She wondered if Keiko knew that Byrum was right next door with his ex.

"He should be here soon. Do you want to come up and wait so that you can say hello?"

"No need to go upstairs to do that. I just saw him."

"Oh?" Keiko asked, looking beyond her to the street.

"Yeah, he's next door."

Keiko smiled over at her.

"I told him I wasn't feeling well. He's probably getting me some soup as well."

"I don't think that's it or at least I don't know."

Keiko cocked her head to the side. She was confused.

"What? How sick am I? You're being weird. Don't be weird. I feel like you're talking in riddles."

"I saw him next door, yes, but he wasn't ordering soup. I'm not sure. I am sure that he's next door with Valencia."

"Who? Valencia? Here in Detroit?"

"Yes. She's right next door. Look, it may be nothing. Did he tell you she was here?"

Keiko didn't respond. What Madison feared happened.

In her bright pink sweat suit and matching crocs on her feet, Keiko walked around her and out of the building. She raced behind her wishing that she'd said nothing. The look on Keiko's face told her that Byrum hadn't said anything about Valencia being in town. Clearly, he knew. She didn't just show up and find him just as he was coming home from a flight to Hawaii. Stirring up trouble was the last thing she wanted to do.

Madison stood behind Keiko as she walked into the deli and stood behind Byrum, who didn't see her coming.

"Hello?" Valencia said to Keiko, causing Byrum to turn around.

Keiko ignored her and looked to him.

"Byrum? I didn't realize you were home. You're here next door," Keiko said calmly.

Madison hated that calm tone of hers. She preferred her friend when she ranted and raved when she was upset. This calm Keiko was a dangerous one.

Byrum stood and turned around to face Keiko.

"Baby, you know, Valencia," he said.

"Baby? Wait, I know you. Your hair is shorter or something, but I definitely know you."

Byrum attempted to do an introduction, but whatever he was going to say, fell on deaf ears.

"Yes, you do know me. You're here in Detroit? Right here where Byrum lives?" Keiko asked.

"I do know you. I recognize your voice. You're his assistant, right? Kima or Kenu or something like that?" Valencia asked. "You're calling your assistant, baby? You're dating her?"

When Byrum turned to address Valencia's blatant attempt at disrespect, Keiko turned and left the deli; Madison followed behind her and back into the condo building.

"Now, wait a minute, sis. You don't know what that was."

"Sure, I do. That was Byrum at a deli with his ex. Who was that man? She looks like him. It may be her father. Why are they here? Why didn't he tell me he was meeting with her? He didn't even say she was in town. If I was feeling better, I would have nastily corrected her disrespect of who I am and what my name is. I'm going upstairs. Are you coming or going?" Keiko asked.

"Are you upset?"

"A little. The sight of that woman and what she did? He shouldn't be entertaining a conversation with her. It was an image of a circus."

Keiko huffed and puffed and headed to the elevator. Madison looked between the door and where Keiko had gone to figure out what direction she should go in. She didn't think Keiko was the jealous type. Something else was going on. She would stay for a few minutes. The minute Byrum showed up, she was out.

Sliding in the elevator next to Keiko, Madison stayed quiet. Neither of them said a word. She could barely hear their breathing.

"I'm sorry I said anything."

Keiko looked her way and then reached to her for a hug.

"There is nothing to be sorry for. I'm not upset at her or him. I trust Byrum. I feel like there is always something going on since Byrum and I fell in love. I don't have the energy for entertaining any additional drama. As for her, I know she can be blatantly disrespectful. I didn't want to drag her from that table and stomp her in her designer clothing. I keep telling people to stop thinking they are dealing with the old Keiko. This new me? I wouldn't drag her for still coming after my man. She has nothing coming, for sure. I could see on her face that she was about to try to make me seem beneath her. I didn't have my Vaseline and sneakers. I'm from that kind of hood."

When Keiko let her go, they doubled over in laughter; for Keiko, with coughing added in.

"Have I told you lately that I love this new you? I feel better now. I don't want to see you hurt."

When they reached Byrum's condo, she followed Keiko inside.

"I don't want to see me hurt either. Trust me, if that ever

happens, it won't be because Byrum is seeing someone else. I trust him to not do that to me, just as I wouldn't do that to him. I'm less concerned about him and whatever was going on in that deli, and more concerned about what my ex-husband is cooking up."

"That's good to know. When can we go back to the resort? I left some dollars in G-strings in that stripper club that I need to get back."

"G-strings? Stripper club? Do tell," Byrum said walking in right behind them.

Madison felt like a third wheel when Byrum and Keiko only had eyes for each other. When neither moved or said anything, she knew it was time for her exit.

"Keiko, eat the soup and feel better. Share some with Byrum. He looks exhausted."

Keiko giggled.

"I always share with him."

"We're good at sharing," he quickly added to the conversation.

Madison headed back to the door.

"The two of you are nasty. I'm talking about food. I don't even want to know what you're talking about. I am loving it though."

"Love you, sis!" Keiko hollered just as she shut the door behind her.

**

"Can we talk?" Byrum asked.

"I think we should," Keiko replied.

199

16

Keiko started to head to the sofa where she'd been sleeping before the call from Madison. Then she realized that Byrum hadn't moved; she knew why. She turned back around and went right into his arms. She wasn't angry at him. That was something she needed to immediately relay. The last woman she would be jealous of is Valencia. Him going back to her never crossed her mind.

"Let me explain what you saw," Byrum said before she could say anything.

With his arms snug around her, she didn't really care. The fact that they hadn't seen each other in a while, all she wanted to do was stand like this; feel him; smell him and love him.

"You can, but it's not necessary."

"No? You seemed upset when you rushed out of the deli. You know you don't have anything to worry about, right?" he asked.

Keiko didn't respond. She simply and happily accepted the soft kisses he loved placing on her lips, her nose, her chin and both cheeks.

She pulled way remembering she may have a cold or the flu.

"I don't want to make you sick if I'm coming down with something."

Byrum laughed and pulled her back to him.

"Baby, the way I'm about to be all up in you will show that I don't care anything about getting the cold or the flu from you. They have medication for that. What I need when it comes to you has no cure. Kissing you is a requirement. I also want to be sure you're good."

"I know. Believe me when I say, me leaving out was for her protection and not me being angry or thinking something was going on behind my back. One thing I remember about her is her defense mechanism is looking for ways to be insulting. It's her flight stance. Women like her used to bother me. At this point in my life, my self-esteem doesn't take a hit from mean girls. She's always been one. She's not a threat. She's more like that nasty gum on the bottom of your shoe that you just can't seem to get rid of. I love you. I know you love me. I have a lot on my mind that is impacting my mood these days. I was surprised to see her sitting in that diner like she was claiming her territory. Cute purse though. I'll give her that. Way too much makeup."

Byrum had to laugh, but didn't do it outwardly. He knew that she could feel his body jerk with laughter.

"You like her purse?"

"Byrum Blackstone, don't you dare think about buying me one of those. I'm not flashy like that. I don't have expensive tastes. I'm still a Coach bag kind of woman. I also love some LV, but not that over-priced stuff."

"I noticed that about you. You also love Pandora charm bracelets. One day, I'll figure out which one's you don't have."

"Feel free to check with any of their stores. They have an account of every one of my charms. Hint, hint," she said and winked.

"I got you, baby. You already know."

"So, now that we are talking about her?"

"Right. Valencia and her dad were here for two reasons. I'll start with the easiest. Her father has been seeing how my brothers and I have been expanding in the business world. There was a big news story done about us. He came with a proposition. He asked for fifteen minutes. I gave that to him because after today, I don't want either of them showing up again."

"The other?"

"Valencia had dreams of reconnecting with me now that her arranged marriage burned to the ground. Her father wanted me to know that he was sorry that he ruined what she and I had before. If I wanted to rekindle my relationship because she's still in love with me, he would be behind it all the way. That's why you walked in and I called you baby. I ended their little chat with turn-downs all around. I would never work with him in business. The Blackstone brothers are doing just fine. As far as Valencia, you already know."

Keiko did know. Curiosity got the best of her when she marched over to the deli. She got her eyeful and then she was fine. Other things are bothering her. Before she filled him in, she first needed something from him that she'd been waiting weeks to get.

A kiss. Not just any kiss, but the most salacious one like what she's been waiting for. With their lips only a whisper away, their breaths mingling close but not touching in order to draw out their desire to be together again, she lifted her eyes to his and knew the minute that he knew. When he finally kissed her, she could feel her cheeks grow warm, her need tinkered on the edge of desperation.

Her heart was beating loudly, her body thumbed with need and desire beyond any comprehension.

"Baby, you feel warm. As much as my ego would love to hear that it's because we're together again, I think you should get back to bed; or back on the couch where I see you've been comfortable. Come on," Byrum said, taking her hand and leading her back to the sofa.

"No, I want to be close to you. You look tired. You have to be after being in the air so much over the past week or so. Is Callum okay?" she asked.

"He will be. I would be making light of it if I said he messed up. He crashed and burned that bridge with Kendra to the ground. She was already gone by the time I got to Chicago to check on what was going on. She was so good for him. I can't believe he tested the boundaries of their relationship by messing around with an ex. I don't know what he was thinking."

"No hope for them?" Keiko asked as she pulled the light comforter back and climbed in bed.

"I doubt it. I get the impression from him that if she said she was done with him, she meant that. Enough of his private life. Let's talk about ours. For starters, whatever Madison brought you in that bag, you need to eat it. Have you eaten today?"

She knew if she admitted that she hadn't he would be angry with her. Byrum is always reminding her to eat while she's trying to keep her life straight.

"I haven't but I will eat some soup."

"That's what she brought? I talked to my mother and she offered to make you some of her homemade chicken noodle soup."

"She did? You were talking to her about me?"

Byrum sat on the edge of the bed.

"Yes. She asked me to invite you to dinner at the house with my family. She wants to get to know you."

Keiko perked up.

"Seriously? What did you say?"

"I told her I would let you know. I also said I would love for you to get to know each other. You are a major part of my life. I know your life is twenty shades wild right now. Let me know if you're not ready. Otherwise, I would really like for you to join me. You already know she's a great cook. You've experienced some of her food when she's brought large spreads that she made to the office. No one tops her southern cooking. It'll be a great time. I wish you could bring Tru, but I know that now isn't the time."

Keiko lowered her eyes. She was suffering by not being able to live her life. There is no reason for her ex to demand that until the new filing is over, he would prefer if she didn't have anyone around Tru. Knowing who Byrum is along with his family, there is no reason for that. Everyone knew that they were good, upstanding and pillars in the community. This life wasn't just about what DeConnor wants. This was her life too.

"You know, I don't think I'm really sick, physically. I think I'm making myself sick because of what I have to deal with when it comes to DeConnor. His demands are ridiculous. He still has to hold all of the cards."

She saw Byrum contemplating something. She could see he had an opinion. She respected how he tried to keep his distance from her situation by allowing her to handle her ex. If they were going to be a real couple, she didn't want anything to come between them, including personal opinions.

"Keiko, tell me this; if DeConnor is filing for full custody because he thinks that we were having an affair before your marriage ended, what about the reason why you left him? Was that brought up in the original divorce proceedings?"

She took a moment to think about that. She realized it never came up; not publicly. She rose up on her knees and moved onto Byrum's lap.

"No. The online cheating and messing around, sex with strippers and expensive call girls, if they still call them that – or rather escorts, didn't come out because he was generous in the divorce. We immediately agreed on equal shared custody of Tru. It never had to go beyond meeting with our attorneys and signing papers."

"Do you still have the proof that you once mentioned to me that you were going to use? You have the records and photos from the private investigator?"

"I have them at my place. Why?"

"Baby, hear me out. This is something to think about. DeConnor is a master at playing dirty. It's time you upped your game and joined him on the same petty level that he lives to be on. Before anything reaches the court, tell him what you have on him. He's so concerned about you and me that he forgets that he actually did mess around on you while you were married. You have proof. He doesn't have any proof about us because it didn't happen. I don't think he wants even a judge to hear about his proclivities. He wouldn't want you to get affidavits from these women about their time with him during your marriage. There is no need for all of this drama. I love you. Just like Valencia, DeConnor has no chance of getting you back, not even through intimidation. If he hurts you in any way, he hurts us. When I say us, I'm speaking of us as a family, which includes Tru. No man should take a child from his mother. Same as if it were a woman – she shouldn't do it either. He used threats to get you back here and back in his life. If you want to really fight back, it's time to issue a few threats of your own. I bet if a private investigator was on him right now, he's still doing the same shady stuff with some questionable ladies. It's up to you. I don't want you to do anything you're not comfortable with. I simply want to see that smile back on your face all the time. I love that you bring goodness into us. I want more for you. Your co-parenting arrangement has worked all this time until he found out about us. I'm sorry about that. It's your call, but I don't want to have to settle for anything less than loving you and you loving me."

She caressed his face, touching her lips to his in a brief kiss.

"No. This is nothing that you would need to apologize for. Loving you and you loving me is everything. I have never, ever been happier. I am happy. I'm just stressed. You're right. He is planning on playing dirty. Every time I think about who he keeps making me turn into, I keep singing, *pop out and show 'em!* That happens to me at least once a day. You're right. I'm not letting him win. Let your mom know that I appreciate the dinner invite and I will be there and so will Tru. My ex doesn't have that kind of power. DeConnor is going to be out of town later this week. I'll plan to talk to him when he gets back. Not about the dinner because that's none of his business. I want to see how far he really wants to carry this."

Byrum stood, sliding her back to the bed. She fake sulked when he moved away.

"I'm going to heat up your soup and whatever else is in the bag. You're going to get in bed to get some rest. As soon as I get a shower, I'm going to join you."

"Oh, yes!"

"No, not that. To sleep. We both need to rejuvenate. We have all day and night together. First you eat, then we sleep. After that, I'll let you determine what direction our desires take us in."

"Oh, I like that. I have to start with food to get to that?"

"Yes, you do," he said, leaning over and offering her his lips again.

"Bring on the soup, baby!" she declared.

17

DeConnor checked his watch for the third time wondering where Keiko was. She was thirty minutes late for meeting him and Tru at the park. Usually when they did the exchange of Tru, if it wasn't at his school, where he now goes to camp for the summer, it was either at his place or hers. When she said she would pick him up from the park, he wondered why she wanted a change in location. Perhaps, she had a play date set up for Tru and meeting at their son's favorite park was most convenient. He was growing impatient. It wasn't that he had any place to go after Tru leaves with her. Truth be told, he was excited about seeing Keiko.

Sitting on the park bench where he could keep his eye on Tru who was playing with kids he knew from school or perhaps camp since they weren't too far from there, he was about to send Keiko a text to see where she was when he saw her walking in his direction.

He admired her from a distance. There was something different about her that he loved. Besides the fact that her new haircut was the sexiest style he'd ever seen on her, he was mad at himself for the many times that she wanted to cut her hair short like this only for him to tell her that he loved it long. He didn't. What he didn't like were the looks from other men that she received like now. His eyes took in others who were admiring her. It wasn't just her gorgeous looks that drew attention her way. There was a new confidence about her that was appealing.

Keiko was an attractive woman. He wasn't the only man to ever notice her. Even now, as she walked in his direction from the parking lot, his eyes landed on her long, beautiful legs. The way her shorter, thick cut swung as she walked made her look like a model on a runway. Her attire was even different each time he saw her. He didn't like his wife being too sexy for men to see; only him. Since the divorce, she was a different woman. Even though they were divorced and he was using filing for full custody of Tru as a way to get her back, he had hoped that the passive Keiko would give in and give their marriage another try. His life wasn't the same without her in it. He knew it would be an uphill battle competing with Byrum. He'd had Keiko first. She was even married to him before. That should give him some upper hand.

He couldn't find a woman as committed and submissive as she was in their marriage. The fact that her personality had changed to a stronger one was the greatest turn on. The way she's been handling him lately caught him off-guard. This new Keiko was hot and sexy. Maybe he could take this time to convince her that they could get out of this new court business if she would come back to him. He stood when she walked up. He told himself to focus on being cordial and not confrontational. There was a saying that you should kill someone with kindness. In this instance, he needed his niceness to work to his benefit.

"Keiko. I was just about to give you a call. You're not usually late."

"Hey. I had a quick errand that ran late. Besides, traffic was a little heavy."

"You look like you're dressed for a night out. You're taking Tru, right? Did I get the days wrong?"

Keiko sat down after waving and smiling to Tru who spotted her when she walked up. He sat next to her. He frowned when she moved to the end of the bench to put some space between them.

"No, you were right. You didn't get his hair cut? Did you forget that you agreed to do that before I picked him up today? We're going to a friend's house for dinner tonight. DeConnor, you had that one job. I'll have to try and get him one before we go to dinner. He wasn't even in camp all day today."

"I did forget. Besides, you didn't say it was because he was going to someone's house. Do I know this friend?"

"Do you need to know the friend? I'm sure you don't share with me every person you take him around. That's too much oversight. I trust you when he's with you; I would appreciate the same courtesy."

"If you must know, there isn't anyone to take him around that you don't know. I'm not seeing anyone like you are. I should be kept in the loop when you have men around my son."

"Men? Don't go there. I don't have *men* around your son. Well, tonight I will. We're going to dinner at Byrum's parents' home. His mother invited Tru and I and we're going."

"You're really going through with continuing to see Byrum, huh? You know, all the drama we're about to go through over custody can be avoided. I told you what you need to do."

"Yes, I know. Your threats don't work on me. If you want to go through with everything, I'm here for it. I'm back in Detroit and ready for anything you throw at me. You are who I expect you to be. I'm waiting to get before the judge. No dealing just with lawyers and paper signing this time. I'm not agreeing to anything that isn't the agreement we already signed."

DeConnor chuckled at her defiance. He hated it, but he never realized how sexy it would look on her. Throughout their marriage, he was used to what he said, is how things went.

"All I ask, in order for this to go away, is for you to consider giving being together again a chance. Tru deserves to have parents who are in the same household."

He felt angst when Keiko laughed at him.

"Tru deserves to see his parents happy, which I am. He deserves to see his parents in love, which I am. It's just never going to be any love between us again. Our focus should be on him and not on me. You can't force me to do things your way by saying that you'll take my son away from me because of what you think you know. Truth is, you don't know a thing about me or what I have with Byrum. If what you want is a fight in court about this, I'm ready."

"You're ready for what? It's not some kind of coincidence that you happen to be sleeping with your boss. You can't make me believe it hasn't been going on longer than you claim."

"If that's the case, why would you want me back? If I cheated on you, why would you want to consider remarrying me? That would make me a cheater. Oh, wait – I wasn't the cheater in our marriage. That would be you. Look, I don't want to drag any of our marriage drama into a court room where everything that is shared will be in the final record. We would have to tell all. Are you ready to do that? I don't have anything that I wouldn't want someone to hear about. You, on the other hand, should be concerned."

DeConnor laughed at her attempt to get one up on him. He was the expert at that, not her. If she wants there to be tension, he had no problem reminding her of her place in his life and in this world when it came to her being a woman. He controlled her every move. He will do so again. First, he needed to get her in line. She needed a reminder of who she was talking to.

"Keiko, you need to think about what you'll lose if you continue on this path of defiance. I know you're trying to exert some form of independence but things won't turn out well. That's all I'm going to say. I could say more, but we're in public. I'm assuming that's why you wanted to meet here in this park instead of me bringing Tru to your place or you picking him up from mine."

"Your display at my apartment at *Silent Whisper* was enough for me to not have discussions with you in private. DeConnor, I'm tired of the back-and-forth. I am more than happy to allow a judge to rule on this new custody thing that you want to push forward. My counter has been filed in court today and I am seeking sole custody of Tru due to your past practices of the kind of women you indulge in. Let's go with that, if that's what you really want. In the meantime, there are a few things that you need to be reminded of."

"Like what?"

He was losing his patience. He was growing agitated. Keiko was trying to control the conversation. Women did not get control. They took what was dished out to them, the way life was supposed to be.

"Like, what you did that led to me filing for divorce. The details of your proclivities with untoward women were never disclosed."

"We agreed that the circumstances weren't warranted because you got what you wanted."

"I did get what I wanted. You're now trying to take that away. I'm not standing or sitting still for that. If you continue this unnecessary fight, I will have my lawyer present the reports and images from all that you were doing, to the court. We're even prepared to present affidavits from several of the women that were caught on camera with you. I'm not playing games with you anymore. You want to have us drag out dirty laundry, let's go. You don't have anything on me because I was not seeing Byrum until his brother's wedding. There is nothing to see there. I love my son. I would give my life for him. As for you, I will not let you have any control over my life that is no longer your business. I am in love with Byrum. We will continue to see each other. Tonight, Tru and I will have dinner with Byrum and his family. They don't need to be vetted. All you need to do is check the news, social media and articles and you'll find only good things about him and his family. There isn't a judge in this land who would find any reason that his family isn't a good one to be around. They are generous, looked upon with high esteem and do a lot for Detroit. Byrum is a wonderful man. He's not Tru's father and he's not trying to take that role from you. He is the man that I love and yes, that's not going to change because you're acting jealous. There is no reason in this world that Tru can't be around Byrum and you know it. You know about him. You've met him. There is nothing else that I need to do in order to keep you in the loop when it comes to our son's life. As for my life, I would appreciate it if you would mind your business."

When she stood to leave, DeConnor sat still, his foot tapping repeatedly on the ground. How dare she, his mind yelled. He couldn't control his anger. He knew his face showed that. Women don't turn their backs to him. Certainly not his ex-wife.

He stood to go after her when to his left, someone placed a large folder on the bench next to him. When he looked up, it was Byrum.

"Let it go, DeConnor. Let me be very clear. You looked like you were about to do something stupid. Don't let that be the last move you make today without something ending up broke. She's not trying to hurt you. She's not trying to keep or take your son from her. I will support her in her fight against you because I love her. I'm sorry you're having a hard time dealing with that. Don't come for my woman; ever. You won't like the response. I let you have your say back at *Silent Whisper*. I saw a man who wanted his ex-wife to conform. She is her own woman. I love that about her. She told me it took her a long time to find herself again. Now that she has, I won't let you hurt her in any kind of way. I've secured the best set of attorneys out of New York to represent her with anything you bring her way. These photos and transcripts that involve you should be handed to your attorneys. If you still choose to proceed, the contact information for Keiko's new team of lawyers is included in this folder. Do you. I allowed you to disrupt my life with Keiko on the island because this issue, at that time, was between you and her. That's no longer the case.

Any fight of hers is my fight too. Trust me, bro, you do not want to go up against a Blackstone. We play to win."

"The next move is yours, playboy," Keiko said facetiously.

DeConnor snatched up the folder and took a quick look at what was inside. Keiko always said she had some kind of proof. He didn't expect to see images of himself with women in living color. Some of the images could hurt him in his career. When his eyes caught sight of Tru coming his way, he closed the envelope and stood. Tru raced to his arms before moving to his mother where he hugged her real tight.

"Hi, Mr. Blackstone," Tru said.

"Tru, it's good to see you again."

"Dad, mom says I'm going to a big house for dinner. Did you know that Mr. Blackstone was mommy's friend?"

DeConnor looked to Keiko and then to Byrum before stooping down to Tru's level.

"I did know. We are happy for her, aren't we?"

"Well, she smiles a lot more because he makes her happy. I'm happy too. Are you coming with us to dinner?"

"No. You go with mommy and have a good time. I know you're going to have fun. Don't overeat if that food is delicious. I'm sure it will be. I will see you in a few days."

"Okay, dad. Mommy, let's go. I'm hungry."

"Hair cut first, young man," Keiko noted.

"Oh, alright."

"Byrum; Keiko," DeConnor said, acknowledging that they were on the same page. "I will reach to my lawyer to be sure she knows the current divorce agreement is fine. No other action is necessary. Are you planning on going back to the island and leaving Tru with me?" he asked.

"No. I need to be a bigger presence in his life here in Detroit, at least for the moment."

"He has a few more weeks of summer left if you'd like to take him and show him the island. Let me know. With his time cut short there with you, I think he'd like to see more of it."

"Are you sure?" she asked. "No more games or threats?" she asked.

"I'm positive. Tru, how would you like to go on another long plane ride with your mom to see the island again? This time, you'll get to stay longer," DeConnor asked.

Tru bounced around on his feet.

"Can I swim in Mr. Blackstone's pool? I didn't get to last time," Tru asked.

"Well, when mommy packs your bag, make sure you take all of your swim trunks. You may need them for all that swimming you'll get to do. I want you to have fun. Just make sure you call me often. I'm going to miss you."

"I'm going to miss you too dad. Mom, are we getting on the airplane today?"

"No, not today. We will soon. Let's get your hair cut and then go to dinner. We can talk about going to the island another time, okay?"

"You promise? I don't like the long ride, but I want to go again."

"Yes, mommy promises that we will go back to the island. Thanks, DeConnor," she said with lighthearted words.

"You play hard and fast and I like that. Byrum, good seeing you again."

Keiko looked to Byrum who put his hand out for DeConnor to shake.

"You'll be seeing a lot of me. Getting along is best for all of us, especially Tru. Agreed?"

"Hard ball. I see why you have succeeded in business. Good luck," he said.

DeConnor turned and walked in the direction of his car, the opposite way that they went. Before reaching his car, he turned back and watched Keiko place her hand in Byrum's as they walked. He knew it was time he moved on. The best man for her had her.

18

Keiko tiptoed into the bedroom and closed the door behind her. After a full day of fun with Tru around the island, she was just as tired as Tru had been. By the time they got back to her apartment, Tru could barely keep his eyes opened long enough to eat dinner and get his bath. Several times, she had to hold his head in her hand in order to finish the bath. If he hadn't spent part of the day in the pool, she would have waited until the morning to get his bath in or maybe a quick shower. She didn't want him in bed without cleaning him off.

When they first arrived, Tru played by himself while she prepared dinner. He had been wide awake, probably from the excitement of the day. He had adjusted well to being back on the island.

She knew the day was over for him when she turned to ask if he'd had enough of the pasta and baked chicken she'd made only to find him asleep at the table. How she managed to get him in the tub and in bed while all still asleep she didn't know. Byrum was a big help with all of that. While he cleaned up the kitchen once he arrived after leaving the resort office, she had tended to Tru. After one week of being back on *Silent Whisper*, her life was back on track. She also had her son here with her which added to her happiness. They had the rest of the summer ahead of them before he would be back with

DeConnor for the beginning of the school year. At least, that was the plan.

Several weeks had passed since they ended the court ordeal. A week after having dinner with Byrum's family, the three of them flew back to the island on his jet. Two days after that dinner, Byrum had flown back to the island to get work done. When she and Tru were ready to fly, he came back to pick them up. Since then, they settled into life on the island. Shew was back to work and Tru was enrolled in camp.

She had spent so much time getting Tru ready for bed that by the time she reached her bedroom and saw Byrum looking like he was asleep as the television watched him, she paused at the door and took all of him in. Never could she have imagined that this would be her life.

Loving Byrum made her heart want to leap out of her chest and just live inside of his. Earlier in the day, after the staff meeting where Byrum gave them all an update on the progress at the resort, he let them know that they were ahead of schedule. They were looking at a grand opening in less than a year; more like early spring. That update brought about a round of applause from everyone. She was just as happy, especially knowing that she was back on the island on a full-time basis. She could even love Byrum without hiding. Everyone had already gotten used to seeing them together. There was no gossip and no one complained of favoritism. It was back to work as usual. What was also back to usual was their insatiable appetites for each other. With no issues or struggles with other people like their exes, their love grew with each day. A lot of it had to do with the vibe of being on the island and at the resort. The more that construction was completed, the more the romantic aura began to take over the entire place. To her delight, she and Byrum were able to spend time in one of the beach cabanas. Sarai had agreed to watch Tru which gave her and Byrum some alone time. They decided to take advantage and get a first-hand experience at what a night in the cabana would be like for the guests. They had made sweet love pretty much all night long. Just when she thought that they were done and were going to get some sleep under the stars, Byrum pulled her close and loved on her again. The full moon, the fire pit, the comfortable round bed with the softest linens she'd ever been on and then an intimate menu made just for lovers, there was no way that wasn't one of the best nights of her life.

During the day, it was business. There was still a lot of work to do and that's where their focus was. She had also started working on her business plan for the virtual assistant business she would one day start. Byrum was there to give her feedback on her plan which she took in and appreciated. The love and support he gave her every day did not go unnoticed. Being appreciated and loved by him returned her belief in love that was unconditional. The island had that impact on them. It was made for lovers. If they did nothing else, they loved.

Before joining him in bed, she locked the bedroom door behind her. She'd unlock it later before they actually went to bed, just in case Tru woke up looking for her. This was a time for them. She knew her son. He was definitely down for the night. Out of excitement, he hadn't napped all day.

"You can always take a picture," Byrum said in a low, relaxed tone as he stretched and turned in her direction.

He was in bed, shirtless with his arms crossed behind his head. The room was dimly lit as soft jazz played from the Bluetooth speaker under the television, no sound coming from it as a movie played. The fact that the movie was The Godfather had her laughing. She boxed the air and Byrum laughed out loud. She knew why.

"I'm already imagining a picture in my head of what's under that blanket. Are you naked underneath or will I have some work to do to get you to that point?" she asked, walking slowly over to the bed.

She was already dressed in a black nightie under her robe. She'd taken it with her to shower in the other bathroom since she'd already used it to help Tru bathe. Her hair was pinned on the top of her head. She was more than ready for what she had in store.

Slipping out of her robe, she slid into bed, sidling right up to Byrum with her arm across his waist and her head on his chest. When his arm came down to hold her close, she sighed with contentment and a potent level of desire.

"Before you slide your hand down there, no, I'm not naked. I wanted to be sure Tru was in bed and asleep with you in here with the door temporarily locked behind you."

"Off," she said and pointed to his lower body.

When Byrum laughed at her one-word demand, she knew he would comply, which he did. As she shifted to give him room, she watched him remove the last barrier that kept her from seeing and feeling all of him. She easily snuggled back up to him.

"Anything for you. Are you happy being back at the resort?" Byrum asked her.

"More than you will ever know. Besides, how could I be anything but happy and excited over the greeting the team gave me on my first day back in the office. There were flowers, balloons and a full lunch spread. It felt good to be back with everyone. Was that your doing?" she asked.

"Only the food. I wouldn't let them cover the cost of that. The balloons and flowers were the idea of the team. I paid the main resort chef extra for that large spread. The team wanted to spread the joy with you returning. They missed you and your leadership. You are a beautiful person inside and out. That's what makes the team work so well; it's not me or their checks, though that helps. It's all you. Besides, you being back means I can save time being in the air to get to Detroit to see you and Tru often. *Silent Whisper* is you. The love and romance connected to this place is a part of you as much as it is a part of me. We were always to fall in love here. That's what desire is all about."

Keiko knew that his words were true.

"I was overwhelmed and on the brink of tears when everyone shared how they love you and I together. I know some said it during my last day before I went back to Detroit. There is no more hiding and sneaking around. Thanks for staying here at my apartment tonight, for the first time, not just this week, but first time ever."

"I have to say that when the resort opens and guests are in quarters like these, they will love how spacious they are. They are most definitely romantic. And when couples need a little space, there are two bedrooms," he jested.

"Not for us though. I don't care how much space you may think you need, if we're under the same roof, we are in the same bed," Keiko shared.

"I hear you, baby. You won't ever have to worry about me wanting to be in a separate bedroom under the same roof.

How the hell would I be able to sleep knowing all this body wouldn't be sidled up to me like you are now."

"I love when we're on the same page. Also, because of you, Tru had one of the best days of his life. I've never seen him this excited. I'm glad he was able to be here for the carnival. I actually enjoyed that myself. I wish you could have spent the entire day with us, but I get that there were some issues with construction. Anything I need to follow-up on tomorrow after I drop Tru at camp before heading to the office?"

"Woman, we are not about to talk about work when I'm laying naked as a jay bird, hard as a boulder and in bed with you in my arms. Anything about that can wait until tomorrow. I'm glad you had time to take him to the pool at my building this morning. Staying here at your place is easier than carting Tru off-site. I didn't want another night of not being with you. This is our second night together since the day after having dinner with my family. I'm still coming down off of the high of the other night under the stars in the cabana with you. We will do that again."

"Count on that. Did I tell you that your mother called me earlier today? She wanted to thank me for the flowers I sent her to thank her and your father for welcoming me and Tru into their house for dinner. I see why you're always stopping by their house to eat when you're in Detroit. It was the best meal I've ever had. I told her that I need her pot roast recipe."

"I haven't talked to her in a few days. She and my dad are coming to the island next weekend to check out the progress we're making. I can't wait for them to see everything. We are still months from our soft opening. I'm just glad you're back here and once again leading your team. We all missed you.

Enough of the chit chat. I missed you. Come here, baby," Byrum moaned out.

She loved the way his voice deepened and his eyes glazed over when he was aroused. His smokey eyes sent chills down her body. Moving so that she straddled his body, she raised her arms when he reached down to remove her clothing, leaving her nakedness to match his.

The sexy whimper from feeling him skin to skin filled the air. It spoke of the pleasure that cascaded through her body when she felt him beneath her hard, thick and ready.

"I've really missed you. I know we had a perfect night under the stars, but I swear every time in your arms feels as good as the first time. I never want this feeling to end."

"I know. Life happens and we have to deal with that. You should already know that my desire to have you seated on me like this and in any way is also on the top of my list. All you, baby," he offered with an encouraging salacious sigh of delight of his own.

As she rose up to take him inside of her body, her hand wrapped tightly around his arousal, she sank down slowly to make sure she rewarded them with the feel of the ultimate sensual connection. As she took him in, a ragged groan of pleasure emitted from them together, at the exact same time. She flexed her hips, moving around to reacquaint her mind, body and soul with his.

"Deep," she sighed. "Damn, you are so deep. I feel you all over."

"Damn, baby," Byrum hissed through gritted teeth. He thrust up with long powerful strokes causing her body to bounce on him deliciously and delightfully.

His tongue flicked out and caressed her nipples, moving his hands over both breasts, holding them snug in his grip. His head moved from side to side, blowing and nipping at her. Her body's response was instantaneous. His thumbs stroked her. She lowered her head for the kiss that awaited her. Her body trembled and quivered with the feel of him deep inside of her building up an intense owning of their love. They rocked together; they loved as one. Her body knew him to be hers. His body claimed her over and over again with each powerful surge into her.

When he slowed their love making, she enjoyed the feel of perfection.

"I love you," she said against his lips. The zing that filled her as his tongue stroked hers over and over was exhilarating. This, she knew was the power of love.

"I love you, too, baby. I love you with everything in me and with every part of me that will forever be joined with you.

His expressions of love, complete with the feel of him and her roaring love for him, her body gave into the pleasure she needed from the moment he arrived. Her heightened sensitivity and stimulated sexual response to him had her hips moving in a wild writhing rhythm that caused her to lose all control. Her mouth opened as she prepared to let go of her release and the most vocal way possible.

Byrum knew it and saved the day. He pulled her head to his and captured the raging sound of her power-filled orgasm. They were not alone. She was thankful that he remembered that. She let her scream be smothered by his kiss.

The sky-high, slicked body rise of an earthquake-like magnitude orgasm rose to the surface as Byrum's body possessed hers. His increased, rapidly surging and mercilessly thrusts into her body was a tantalizing rhythm that had them both on the brink of shattering together, for her, this would be a succeeding second one in a manner of seconds.

In a quick moved that surprised and delighted her, Byrum flipped their bodies so that he was on top. With her legs spread wide, he moved them to a rested position in his arms. Her body was open for his and her enjoyment.

Byrum pumped and rocked into her until their bodies calmed after their mutual release shot through them and then set them free. Byrum raised his head and locked eyes with her even as he growled out his pleasure, mixing it with her sounds of immense satisfaction.

Minutes later, their bodies finally did calm in the afterglow of passion that didn't spare any part of them where they bonded wantonly.

"Our desire is so potent; so fiery," she said softly against Byrum's neck.

"I think I'd categorize it as being within the heart-attack zone," he quizzically shared.

Byrum bent and planted gently placed kisses against her forehead before lowering her legs and settling between them.

"I want to fall asleep just like this, with you inside of me."

"Your desired wish, as usual, is my command, except, the door is locked," he reminded her.

"I know. Which one of us has legs that could make it to the door right this minute?" she playfully asked.

"Right. Give me about ten minutes for the blood to flow back to my brain so that I know how to walk again," he chuckled. "While we're waiting, I want to ask you about something."

Keiko lifted his head so that they were looking into each other's sexually drive haze-covered eyes.

"I'm listening," she offered.

"What do you think about moving in with me for the remainder of the time we're on the island. As much as I love being here tonight, I really don't want to keep running into the team considering most of them live onsite. I want more privacy for us. I know with Tru here we need to be mindful of what he hears and sees. I don't want to mess that up. You're the parent, something I've never been. What's the protocol with that? If it's not a good time, I get that. I just want you to think about it."

Keiko shifted a little and lowered her legs, but locked them around his waist, their bodies still connected.

"I don't have to think too hard on that. I love the idea. Tru isn't a problem. I will sit him down and talk to him about that. I'm not sure he remembers much about me and his father living under the same roof. He knows I love you and that you love me. I have talked to him about that. When do you want to do this?"

"As soon as possible. I know Tru is here. What are your thoughts about that? My condo has plenty of room. He would have his own space. I don't want us shifting between here and there all the time."

"I agree. I was actually thinking about asking DeConnor to let Tru stay through the end of the year. He's only in kindergarten. The schools here are great. It wouldn't be much of a change for him at this young age. I'm not sure I can handle letting him go after being here for the rest of the summer. Before bringing this up to you, I was thinking of a way to broach the subject with his father. I didn't want to do that without talking to you. You keep saying we are a packaged deal. I want you involved in decisions that impact all three of us."

"Baby, I'm glad you brought this up. I think it's a great idea. He's been very cordial and agreeable lately. I believe you're in a great place. He has to know what being away from your son does to you. Maybe he will be open to it. I'm with you all the way. Do what you need to do. Consider me in your corner with every decision you make. *Silent Whisper* is our home right now. That means that in a way, it's Tru's home as well. If you want him here, that's a non-conversation. It's always a yes for me."

Keiko pulled him closer to her sweat-covered body.

"I love you. I don't know how I got this lucky to be the face of your desire. You're always making sacrifices for me. What can I do for you?" she asked. "You do so much to make sure I'm good; to make sure I'm happy. Are you good? Are you happy?"

"Keiko, I have never, ever been happier. I never thought I could be this happy. You are Tru are my life. What impacts you, impacts me. I don't ever plan to replace his father in his life, but me, you and Tru are a family."

Keiko caressed his face; then his head and then his back. She quietly gave thanks for the man in her arms.

"You've been through so much. Are you sure about us? About me and Tru?"

"I'm better than sure. I love you. I love Tru. I love us. There is no cost to DeConnor's cooperation anymore. I'm open enough to put him up in one of the rooms here if he wants to visit with Tru if that will make negotiating with him easier. I would do any and everything for you and Tru. Now, I think I have feeling back in my legs. I'll get up and unlock the door. I say we put some pajamas on, just in case we get a little visitor before daylight."

Keiko moved with him. She raced into the bathroom to quickly wash her body. Byrum did the same after her. Instead of putting her nightie back on, she slipped on a tank top and a pair of shorts. Byrum reached in his bag and pulled out checked pajama bottoms and a white t-shirt. She went to check on Tru before turning all the lights out, shutting off the television and turning the volume to the music down, but not off. Back in bed and in Byrum's arms, she fell asleep to his utterances of how he was the lucky one to be able to love her and to have her love him. What they shared wasn't just his desire for her, but also her desire for him. They were absolutely a perfect match.

Epilogue
One year later at 'Silent Whisper'

Byrum waved Tellum and Cheyenne over to the seats he held for them in order to enjoy a battle of the bands concert that was being hosted at *Silent Whisper*. A month after the grand opening, the resort was full with excitement for the event. Keiko tapped his shoulder so that he would change seats with her, allowing her the chance to sit next to Cheyenne. Where they could have sat in VIP seating, Byrum wanted them to experience the concert from the vantage point of their general stay guests. They were minutes from the lights going down as the event host made her way to the stage to get things started.

"Where's Callum?" Byrum asked Tellum when he and Cheyenne took their seats.

"He's at *Quiet Whisper*. He was planning to join us but he had some friends who were coming to the island to hang out with him for a few days. You know what it's like when Lucas finds time to get away from touring to catch up with him. I told him I would let you know that he wasn't coming," Tellum said.

Byrum leaned over and hugged Cheyenne after she and Keiko greeted each other.

"Can I?" Byrum asked Cheyenne pointing.

"Of course. Uncles and godfathers are always welcome. I can't wait for y'all to meet this little lady," she said before he reached out and placed his hand over her growing belly.

"How far along are you?" Keiko asked.

"I'm officially six months as of yesterday."

"Are you ready to be a father, Tellum?" Byrum asked him once they'd all settled in.

"Man, this is the longest nine-months in the world. I'm more than ready. After her miscarriage, we're excited that there are no issues this time. That was a hard time for us all. That only made me want to be a father even more. I'm already making plans to get baby number two in the making before this one is a year old," he joked.

"Don't listen to your brother. When he's had night after night of not sleeping, feedings and diaper changes, he won't be so excited about another one so soon," Cheyenne kidded.

"How is Tru?" Cheyenne asked Keiko. "I may need to all you with some motherly advice."

"Call me anytime you want. Tru is doing good. He's actually with my parents in Boston while I'm here for this week with Byrum. No longer living on the island full time is an adjustment. I think Tru is more upset than I am. He went to school here until December and loved it. He wasn't ready to go back to Detroit. I reminded him that we would travel back and forth. He was supposed to be with his father, but he is on a trip with his new girlfriend."

"Tru is getting tall. Before we left to come back here, I had to raise the seat on his bicycle because his legs are getting longer," Byrum added.

"I guess mom actually got a grandchild even before Cheyenne got pregnant by way of Tru. I called her a few weeks ago from Secret Whisper and Tru was spending the night with her and Pop. That had to be fun," Tellum said.

"Bro, when I tell you that mom loves him as if he was her

actual grandson, I mean that. She gets excited when she gets to spend time with him. Out of the blue when we stopped by for a visit and Tru was with us, we were talking about a movie Keiko and I wanted to go see. She told us to go. She would keep Tru. That turned into him having so much fun with them that he asked to spend the night. Dad even ran to the store to grab him some pajamas and other stuff he would need so that Keiko wouldn't have to go back to our place to get him a change of clothes. At least we get to see first-hand how good they're going to be with your new bundle after Cheyenne gives birth," Byrum said.

"That's the truth," Tellum acknowledged. "She is a big help to Cheyenne now. Life is good?" he asked Byrum.

"Damn right it is!" Byrum shouted as heads turned to look in his direction. When people saw who he was, the berating that they would have given someone else turned into cute waves of hello.

The lights in the concert arena went down, signaling the start of the show. Byrum knew they would finish catching up at dinner after the show which was already planned out.

Before he could get comfortable to enjoy the evening, Byrum's phone vibrated in his pocket. Keiko looked at him to signal that if it's work-related, he should ignore it.

"Baby, it's Callum. He said he needed to speak to me and Tellum, right now. There were about thirty exclamation points added to the end of the text."

"Yeah, I got the same text. Bro, let's step out. He knows we're at the concert. It's eight in the morning there in Hawaii. It must be important. We'll be right back," Tellum said.

Byrum followed him out into the main lobby.

"I wonder what this is about?" Byrum asked opening up

the video chat app to talk with Callum. His brother answered on the first ring.

To say that Callum looked ragged would be an understatement. He looked like he was carrying the weight of the world on his shoulders.

"Bro, what's going on? Why the urgency?" Tellum asked.

Byrum looked closer into the screen.

"Are you at a hospital? It looks like a hospital lobby behind you. What the hell is going on?"

"I need you and Tellum to meet me here in Hawaii as soon as you can. I wouldn't usually ask you to uproot your lives and hop on a plane, but I need you here. Pop is already on his way from Detroit," Callum pleaded.

Byrum and Tellum both heard and saw the urgency. They were concerned that Callum had another drinking binge, which he promised them that he would stop doing after the incident with his ex, Kendra over a year ago.

"Callum, tell us what's going on. Are you hurt? Did something happen to someone on the construction site at the resort? Talk to us," Tellum said.

"Nothing like that. Kendra arrived here today," Callum explained.

"Okay. Is she okay?" Byrum asked.

"She is but my sons aren't," Callum explained.

Tellum and Byrum looked to each other and mouthed the word, sons.

"Callum, what are you talking about? Sons? You don't have any sons. Have you been drinking?" Byrum questioned.

"Let me start over. When Kendra and I broke up a little over a year ago, I didn't know she was pregnant. She didn't know either," Callum started to explain further.

"When did you find out?" Tellum asked.

"A few hours ago. She called me last night and asked if I was in Detroit. I told her I was here in Hawaii with some friends. She asked if she could come here to talk to me. Of course, I agreed. I haven't spoken to her since she broke up with me. I tried for over six-months with no response from her at all. I didn't know she was pregnant. When she landed at the airport, I met her there. You know I was shocked to see her with two babies along with her mother and sister. She ran everything down to me."

"What? That she had two whole ass babies and never told you? Never told this family? Who does that?" Tellum asked.

"You'd be surprised how pissed off a woman can actually be," Byrum said.

"True, and she was. The issue is, both boys are sick. They are almost four months old and have diagnosed congenital heart defects. They have complex valve or heart rhythm disorders. They're going to need surgeries. As their father, I'm going to give blood for the surgeries they'll need. You should see them all tiny and sick. They have feeding and breathing issues, among other things. You should see them. They look just like me, before you ask."

"Neither of us were going to ask that. If you already know, that's all we need to hear. Callum, you had that problem as a baby. Do you remember mom telling us the story of how you made it through that touch and go time in your life?"

"I know. I told Kendra that. I'm scared for them. Pop just called and said he talked with some friends of his in the medical field who put him in touch with a Dr. Clayton Myers out of Texas. The doctor told him to get the twins to Texas Children's Hospital as soon as possible. When he told him the babies were here in Hawaii, he patched Pop in to a doctor from that hospital who said before we put them on another flight, he wanted to check them over. Doctor Myers is on his way here to Hawaii along with his wife, who is also a doctor. We'll then get the babies to Texas for care, if need be. He believes they can get the care here considering who we are. He knows that we can afford to bring in any doctor from anywhere in the world that we need."

"Kendra flew them all the way to Hawaii?" Tellum asked.

"She was scared and didn't trust anyone. She said the doctor who was treating them in Las Vegas wasn't as forthcoming as she thought he should be. Even though the issue was diagnosed, she felt like they were using the boys' condition for research. That frightened her. Her team coach helped her get a medical flight to Hawaii after she told her that I was here and she needed to get them to their father; the only man she trusted to help her look after their care. She looks like she hasn't slept in months. Not just because she has twins but because of worry. Look, I know I'm asking a lot, but can you get here for support? I really need my brothers; I need my family."

"How are they right now?" Byrum asked.

"They were given strict instructions for the boys from Dr. Myers. I was finally able to convince Kendra and her family to get some sleep. It took a lot to get them to leave the hospital. I promised her that I would not leave their side until she got back. They're staying in a part of Silent Whisper that is already complete. I was going to do a hotel but I figured they would get more rest there because there is only staff on the premises who promised me that they would look after Kendra and her family as if they were their own family. Look, can you get here?"

Tellum stepped away and pulled out his phone.

"We're calling the airport right now. As soon as the jet can get us there, you'll see us. Hold it together. If a doctor is flying out, I'm sure he's the best. Tell Kendra we're on our way."

"I'll see you when you get here. I've got sons. Can you believe that?"

"I can. You loved that girl or there wouldn't be any babies," Byrum said.

"As quiet as it's kept, I've always and only loved Kendra. She'll never believe that. Our kids brought us back together. I'm never letting go; not ever," Callum declared.

"I'm happy to hear that, but don't forget what you did to make her leave you. I don't think she'll forget even with the boys being sick. What are their names?" Byrum asked.

"Finn and Liam. They don't have my last name, but they will. The only thing that matters right now is getting them healthy."

"Bro, you overcame the same defect and so will they. I need to go and make Cheyenne and Keiko aware that we need to get to Hawaii. We'll take my jet and leave Tellum's here for them to return home to Detroit. Hold on. We're on our way. Our phones are on or call the phone in the jet. If we need to get anything and everyone there to care for our nephews, a simple text will do."

"I love them, Byrum. I love my boys and I just met them."

"And Kendra?"

"I have to find a way to make up what I did to hurt her. I can't have my boys getting healthy and she walks back out of my life. I have them; I still want her. That thirst I once told you I had for her that could never be quenched by another woman? It's true. I didn't realize it until I saw her in a helpless state. Then I saw my boys and knew that I messed our lives up by being messy. I'm putting all that behind me. My focus has to be on my life with my sons and if Kendra could ever forgive me, my life with her."

"Bro, don't worry. That thirst you've always had for Kendra won't go away. I believe it will be a part of what brings you back together. If you want her, you fight for her. Just like we want Finn and Liam to fight to stay here with us, with this family, have that same fight in you to win your family. There is no better place to do that than at Quiet Whisper. We're on our way," Byrum said.

The call ended at the same time that Tellum's did with their pilot.

"We ready?" Tellum asked.

"Let's roll. A Blackstone is in trouble. We ride before dawn!" they said together as they sprinted back inside to alert their women.

**

Callum went back into the hospital room where his sons were hooked up to so many machines with wires everywhere that he couldn't stop the tears that rolled down his face even if he tried.

"Daddy is here. I'm never leaving you," he said.

"Are you?"

Callum turned and his eyes met Kendra's.

"You're back already?" he asked.

"Are you?" she asked.

"Am I what?"

"Are you here for them? I mean, not just because they're sick."

"I am here for them now that I know about them. I'm here for you too."

"Callum, I don't need you to be here for me. I need you to be here for our sons. There is no you and I anymore. I hope you get that. We are one when it comes to them. As for us, nothing has changed."

Before he could answer, Kendra stepped away when a nurse walked by. He turned his attention back to his sons. He leaned close to them where they laid in a clear glass hospital cradle together.

"We will be a family and that includes your mother. I knew it the minute she got off the plane with the two of you. I messed up not realizing what I had with her. I promise you that I will fight with everything in me to get her back. I thirst for her. I always have and I always will. You have to get better so that you can help me convince her that I'm not that Callum anymore. In fact, I'm the Callum who has two sons. Fight to stay here with us and I promise you that I will fight to get our family together."

Before he could say another word, signals and sirens around the boys began to go off as doctors and nurses raced into the room. He cried when they asked him to step out of the room where he found Kendra shaking uncontrollably in the doorway. He pulled her away with him and held her tight. Thankfully, she didn't fight him. They needed to reserve their energy to fight for the lives of their sons. At the same time, he was also fighting for him and her.

As more medical staff raced into the room, Callum hoped his family could get to Hawaii and do it fast. He and Kendra needed them. The real revelation was, he now knew how much he has always wanted, needed and desired Kendra; only her.

Now was the time that he got serious about life and love and faced his real truth. His life hasn't been the same since she left him. His goal now is to prove to her that they could have forever if only she could forgive him.

*About the 3rd and final installment in the Island Embers series, **Thirst for You***

Callum Blackstone did the unforgiveable. He was caught with his ex-girlfriend by his then girlfriend, Kendra Grimes. A year after their relationship ended, Kendra showed up asking for help for their twin boys that he didn't know he had. Putting their issues aside, they focus on getting their sons the medical help they need.

As they began to heal, Callum knew that in order to get Kendra back in his life so that he could be a full-time father to his sons, he had to work on a secret, quiet plan of love, adoration and untamed lust to get her to trust him again. There was no better place to do that than on the island of Hawaii at his new resort, *Quiet Whisper*. It was a magical place that anything wished for could be made true. He was counting on everlasting love being the end result. Winning over Kendra's heart again wouldn't be easy. After leaving him once, love is what he hoped would bring her back to him in one of the most beautiful places in the world. He was up for the challenge because his thirst for her has never quenched.

Preorder your copy of *Thirst for You*, the last book in the *Island Embers* series, today at www.cherylbarton.net

Get ready for a new series based out of Las Vegas, also known as *Sin City*. First up in the four-book series, *House of Cards*, will be *Ace of Spades*.

Asia "Ace" Wingate is being given the chance of a lifetime to go from barely making it, to living a lavish life in the city that showed her that using what she has to get what she wants became her mantra. When she meets Dakota Croft, a Las Vegas "Gigolo", she gets more than she bargained for. Just when she thinks she's playing him like a masterful card shark, she discovers that she's the one with her cards stacked on the table and Dakota is the man who has a plan to topple it over until it comes falling down.

One steamy night after another is the name of Ace's game to get to what she wants; ten million dollars. Dakota is playing a different game. His is called, win, never lose and only withdraw when she's satisfied because he's playing for keeps.

Come with Ace on a rollercoaster ride in a game of money, power and respect to see if the woman who usually wins can outsmart the one man she underestimated.

Book 1, Ace of Spades, in the *House of Cards* series, is available for preorder at
www.amazon.com/dp/B0DSZGZYDG

Following, *Ace of Spades*, get ready for the stories of her siblings in, *Jack of Hearts, Queen of Diamonds* and *King of Clubs*.

Sin City will never be the same again with the Wingates on a mission to make Las Vegas bow down and salute them as they make it to the top by any sexy means possible!

Never Can Say Goodbye

Book editor, Taryn Novack turned the idea of falling at someone's feet into her personal nightmare. She'd met attorney, Adrian Jarreau a few times in her aunt's New York Apartment building and found the man irresistible. His hard body wasn't the only 'hard' part of him that she was able to lay her eyes on when she tripped and fell at his feet with him dressed only in a towel wrapped around his hips and nothing else. She could have gotten away with her dignity in place until she decided to look up from his feet to...

Adrian knew that Taryn had been avoiding him since that fateful day that he couldn't remove her and his most embarrassing moment. With her being back in New York after the passing of her aunt, they are thrusts together in more ways than one. Moment gone, their whirlwind affair is about to come to an end and she's set to return to Paris. Can she say goodbye and walk away from him without looking back or ever looking up again?

Secure your copy of "Never Can Say Goodbye" on Kindle Unlimited in May, 2025.

Hunger for You, Book 1 of the *Island Embers* series

Tellum Blackstone was entranced the moment his eyes landed on Cheyenne Reddick and her magnetic beauty. In her eyes, arms, and heart, he thought he'd found forever. A rift between their fathers had him questioning what kind of real love could be torn apart with a line drawn in the sand.

Cheyenne never thought that she would meet the perfect man until she did in Tellum. He exuded the kind of charm, kindness, and simmering heat that had her mind, body, and soul sizzling like no man had ever done before. To her dismay, a ticking time bomb of epic proportion, in the form of her father, brought about an ultimatum for her to choose a man she loves from a family he detests or lose his love and support forever.

At Secret Whisper, a romantic island resort owned by Tellum, Cheyenne finds that his passion-infused hunger for her easily penetrated her paper-thin resistance. Their desire for each other reignited an insatiable appetite that no woman in her right mind could fight.

Tellum put his all into their red-hot kisses and explosive days and nights of seduction. He needed to find a way to overshadow the risk they were taking in discovering if their love was worth fighting for.

Catch up on book 1, Hunger for You
www.amazon.com/dp/B0CQZG6CXK

The Brothers of Chi-Town series

I Can't Let Go, Book 1

Carter Garrison vowed to love, honor and cherish his wife, Sienna, forsaking all others, something he forgot to do during a weekend of fun, bad company and poor judgement.

Sienna Garrison never dreamed her college sweetheart, Carter, whom she pledged her life to, would break her heart and when he did, she moved out and moved on - or tried to. What better occasion is there than a friend's wedding to stir up old feelings and memories of love, intense passion and nights of sensual titillation. Gazes from across a room after almost two years apart revealed depths of love that had never died.

Seeing Sienna again reminded Carter of what he'd lost and he vowed to never let go by doing whatever he could to get his wife back even if it included begging and pleading.

Is Sienna ready to forgive and take a chance on life again with the only man she'd ever really loved?

When Carter brings on the charm and turns up the heat, no woman is immune, especially Sienna.

Swagger and Baggage, Book 2

It's not a coincidence that casino owner, Torrence Allen, ran into his college sweetheart, Reese Michaels again; it's fate. As his memories unfold, he had tried everything to keep her in his life and his bed back then and failed at both. She wasn't ready for him then, but he hopes she is ready for him now.

Reese Michaels never thought she'd see Torrence again. Their split in college was dramatic and hurtful and still, no man had been able to win her heart. She considered herself the permanent third wheel to friends who had found love and marriage. Their whirlwind affair, quickly turned into love just as it suddenly crashed and burned when a woman shows up to claim Torrence as hers. When it's also revealed that this woman isn't the only 'other woman', Reese finds herself left with a broken heart, shattered love, and dreams of forever beyond her reach. How did she not know about the other part of Torrence's active and amorous life?

Torrence isn't ready to give up on having Reese in his life after his deceit. He finds himself in the fight of his life to finally have the love and commitment he wanted only with her. His swagger had always won women over, but it's his baggage that's causing his life to spiral out of control and he could once again find himself without the woman he has always loved.

Claiming His Child, Book 3

Business magnate Dexter Patterson refused to let anything keep him from checking off all of the boxes equating to achievement in life to prove that though he came from a rough childhood on the south side of Chicago, he still thrived and became a success. Looking around at those closest to him, Dexter found that he was still missing something...Love.

When aspiring model, Alyssa Kincaid met Dexter, she couldn't get enough of his sexual magnetism, fiery nights of passion, and secret rendezvous. She thought they were headed toward forever when a surprising call from him ended what they had causing her to leave Chicago, taking with her a secret.

Dexter thought that no woman could ever tame him, not even Alyssa who entranced him with her sexy body, smoky, sultry voice and untamed desire. Too little, too late, he realized he'd made a mistake by walking away and then she was gone. Time and distance didn't diminish the chemistry between them and the child Alyssa carried and never told him about had him in the fight of his life to win back her heart and the chance to have the family he'd always wanted.

Will Alyssa continue to curse kismet when Dexter suddenly reappears in her life or will she believe that his yearning for her isn't just because of their child, but because when she left Chicago, she took his heart with her?

Always Bet on Black, Book 4

Sexy, debonair, Delvin "DJ" "Black" Michaels, left Chicago as a man in search of a better life than the one he had where everyone knew him as "Black". He met a woman, fell in love, and then she turned out to be someone he didn't really know when her scandalous life ruined his career.

Avalon Hart had lived her life on the edge, making do the best way she knew how even if it meant scheming men out of their hard-earned money. She learned how to survive from the streets and she was a woman who had a way with men that got her whatever she wanted, that was until she encountered DJ Michaels in Chicago, a man from her past whom she had once easily swayed to her desires. She realized early that the man she encountered in New York had grown immune to her tricks, even the ones she learned how to do in bed that he loved so much.

DJ and Avalon are on a roller coaster ride to love and neither knew it. He had a lot to lose if he let Avalon get too close to him again. This time, whatever she was plotting, he was ready to take her down, even if it meant losing his heart in the process.

He was betting on "Black" for the win, but so was Avalon, in her own way. There was no telling who would end up on top, but one thing was for sure – the road to getting there was going to be filled with hot, sexy fun, a pair of handcuffs and a whole lot of sensuality that neither could resist!

It Takes Two to Tangle, Book 5

Councilman Tucker Glass, a native of Chicago, has set his eyes on the biggest prize, that of Mayor of the city he has loved all of his life. At thirty-nine, his career spans back many years as a City Council member and then most recently, as City Council President. His resume reads like a ratings-topper novel full of accomplishments that make him more than qualified for the job, but what he wants to avoid is the drama that could block his path to the mayor's mansion. He's always been a strait-laced politician, but his personal life could spawn a real-life reality show complete with hair pulling, tongue-lashing and accusatory finger pointing which would all occur in the first episode. Tucker wasn't expecting his past to come back to haunt him just as he'd found the woman who was making his life complete. He would do anything to keep her in his life, but is he willing to give up his run for the mayor's office to keep that love in-tact? Nichelle Michaels didn't know that love could be so right until she met and fell in love with Tucker Glass, a man fourteen years older and wiser than her, but who showed her how a man should treat a woman, and that's after she spent the past year testing the water between how a man loves and how a woman loves. Now that she knows what she wants, a woman from Tucker's past could ruin her perfect love. Tucker and Nichelle are in love, but is he willing to risk his chance at being Mayor because his ex-wife, or the woman he thought was his ex-wife, wants to now be First Lady of Chicago? Was he really ready to tangle with a woman who specialized in drama every day on television as the star on the nation's number one reality show? Tucker may be ready for Chicago, but is Chicago ready for the drama that comes along with the popular politician?

Crashing Into Love, Book 6

His name is Joseph Kincaid and while most call him Joey, the women of Chicago call him a variety of sexy epithets that are too salacious to utter in public. He's a professional wrestler who is unmatched in the ring, untamed in his response to confrontation and unleashed when it comes to his bedroom proclivities, bringing women pleasure beyond their amorous fantasies.

For the second time in her life, Marlow Warren was responsible for an accident that altered someone's life. The first time, she ran to avoid bringing disgrace to her family while hiding from her past, but this time, she's all about making amends to the man whose life she ruined.

Everything changed when Joey and Marlow's lives collided. It wasn't all bad. Hurt, anger and unending apologies turned into lust, desire and unbridled cravings, something neither of them could fight. When Marlow's past arrives in a threatening way, Joey knew he would risk his life to protect her because he was now fighting for more than a future back in the ring; he was ready to fight for love.

Carlos Kincaid is an irresistible, rugged loner who is the epitome of that good guy who finishes last when it comes to women. His life is finally on track when Everly Robinson, his Achilles' heel returns to Chicago to turn his world upside down. She stirs up memories of their inexhaustible, hot, steamy, lust-filled nights that he thought were long gone.

Everly chose the wrong man one time too many in her life. She finds herself on the run from two dangerous men, one who conned her into leaving the only love she's ever known and the other whom she calls her father. In desperate need of help, she escaped a mental and physical prison to go in search of the one man she trusts and has always loved.

Carlos is frustrated that old feelings could lead him back into the arms of the woman he needed to hate in order to move on. He couldn't tell if her story was filled with lies or truths. Against his better judgement, he's ready to risk his heart and his life for a woman who once betrayed him and his love.

Brothers of Chi-Town Series
I Can't Let Go
Swagger and Baggage
Claiming His Child
Always Bet on Black
It Takes Two to Tangle
Crashing into Love
Leaks, Lies, Lust and Love
Love's Gamble

Get the entire five-book series, The Sullivans of Montana, now available for your reading pleasure. at

https://www.amazon.com/dp/B09M41D76N?binding=kindle edition&ref=dbs_dp_rwt_sb_pc_tkin

The Sullivans of Montana
Home for Thanksgiving
The Way You Love Me
On the Right Track
Three's a Crowd
The Law of Love

Also by Cheryl Barton
www.cherylbarton.net
Upcoming Novels
___Romance___

__Sister Act__
An Unexpected Destiny
For You I Will
More Than Friends

__Bachelor Series__
Bachelor Not for Sale
A Designed Affair
A Perfect Combination
Love at Last

__A Lovers' Heart Series__
Heartthrob
Heartbeat
Heartbreaker

__Island Embers__
Hunger for You
Desire for You
Thirst for You

__Amorous Occupations__
The Artist
The Bookkeeper
The Chef
The Dancer
The Electrician

Stand Alone Romance

Snowbound
Cupid's Arrow
One Wish
His Halloween Promise
Holly for Christmas
A Better Man
Bossy
Un-Break My Heart
Love on Top
Take a Knee
Love at First Sight
My First Love
Black Love
A Younger Man
One Moment in Time
The Lake House
True Lies or True Love
When I Think of You
And Then There Was You
Baby, Come Back
Unforgettable
The Power of Seduction
Seize the Moment
A Christmas Wish
It Should Have Been You
The Christmas Layover
The Sweetest Revenge
The Sweetest Temptation
The Diner
Dashing Through the Snow
A Trick and a Treat
Love Therapy
Mister Christmas

Upcoming Romance Releases

Sons of a Sullivan

Wrath of a Sullivan

Upcoming Urban Drama

Amerikka: Justice or Revenge

Christian Romance Series

When God Says Yes
Rescue Me
Release Me
Restore Me

Inspirational Series

Encouraging Words From One Sister to Another
One Sister Away, Volume 1
One Sister Away, Volume 2
One Sister Away, Volume 3
One Sister Away, Volume 4

Inspirational Standalone
A Letter to My Mother
Straightening Her Crown

About the Author

Cheryl Barton lives in Maryland and in her spare time she loves to read espionage, crime and romance novels, cook, watch Sci-fi movies, spend time with family and friends and enjoy Maryland steamed crabs.
Cheryl is the author of over forty romance novels, four inspirational novels and is proud of six book compilation projects with several other incredible women.
Cheryl was a 2019 Finalist for the Emma Award given by Romance Slam Jam and a 2018 Finalist for the Literary Trailblazer of the Year award by the Indie Author Legacy Award. Cheryl is a member of Maryland Romance Writers at https://marylandromancewriters.com/our-members/member/244/

Cheryl's books are available on her website as well as www.bn.com, www.amazon.com and www.kobo.com

Connect with Cheryl Barton
Author Cheryl Barton website
www.cherylbarton.net
Amazon Author Page
www.amazon.com/author/cherylbarton
Instagram: @cherylbartonauthor
Facebook: @authorcherylbarton
Threads: @cherylbartonbooks@threads.net